'Is that wh_____t you're a nu_____k book?'

He had his hands on her forearms and she couldn't move, but she raised her head defiantly, looking him full in the face.

'Actually, yes.' And she made sure he knew she meant it. She waited for his temper to rise, but he considered her drily, his head to one side.

'Some girls wouldn't mind that,' he said softly. 'Being wined and dined with no strings attached is what plenty of career women call for these days. No messy complications or irritating ties.'

She didn't know quite how to answer that. 'You have an answer for everything, don't you?' she muttered crossly. Her voice wasn't as acidic as she would have liked, mainly because with the palms of her hands pressed against his chest so hard she could feel the beat of his heart, and the smell and feel of him all around her, her head was beginning to spin.

Helen Brooks lives in Northamptonshire and is married with three children. As she is a committed Christian, busy housewife and mother, her spare time is at a premium, but her hobbies include reading, swimming, gardening and walking her two energetic, inquisitive and very endearing young dogs. Her long-cherished aspiration to write became a reality when she put pen to paper on reaching the age of forty, and sent the result off to Mills & Boon®.

Recent titles by the same author:

THE PARISIAN PLAYBOY
CHRISTMAS AT HIS COMMAND
THE GREEK TYCOON'S BRIDE

MISTRESS BY AGREEMENT

BY
HELEN BROOKS

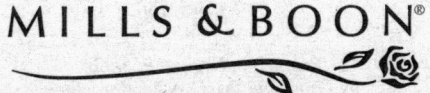
MILLS & BOON®

MILLS & BOON and MILLS & BOON with the Rose Device are registered trademarks of the publisher.

First published in Great Britain 2003
Harlequin Mills & Boon Limited,
Eton House, 18-24 Paradise Road, Richmond, Surrey TW9 1SR

© Helen Brooks 2003

ISBN 0 263 83315 1

Set in Times Roman 10½ on 12 pt.
01-0903-52150

Printed and bound in Spain
by Litografía Rosés, S.A., Barcelona

CHAPTER ONE

'MISS MILBURN? Mr Ward is here for his ten o'clock appointment.' Rosalie's secretary's disembodied voice from the intercom was not as calm and businesslike as usual, and Rosalie knew why, having met the said Mr Ward at a dinner party a few weeks earlier.

She glanced at her neat gold wrist-watch. Eight minutes to ten; he was early. She forced herself to breathe deeply before saying, 'Ask Mr Ward to wait a few moments, please, Jenny.'

'Yes, Miss Milburn.'

The intercom clicked goodbye and Rosalie sank back in the big leather chair, her heart racing. This was stupid; this was so, so stupid. What on earth was the matter with her? She had been like a cat on a hot tin roof since Kingsley Ward had made the appointment a week ago— or rather his secretary had liaised with her secretary, to be exact.

Of course she could have *insisted* he see one of the other three partners in the firm of chartered quantity surveyors she was part of, after her polite message—again via the two secretaries—that she was terribly busy but had arranged for Mr Ward to see a colleague had been turned down flat.

Mr Ward was quite happy to wait until she was available, his secretary had told Jenny, and there was no question of seeing someone else. Miss Milburn had been personally recommended, and Mr Ward *always* went on personal recommendation.

And now he was here. Rosalie glanced nervously round the big, light-filled office that tended to be her home from home with the long hours she worked. She even slept on the couch that occupied one corner when the occasion warranted it. Kingsley Ward was here and it was only at this precise moment that she acknowledged the meeting had been weighing on her spirit like a ton of bricks. It wasn't even as if they had got on that evening at Jamie's house—just the opposite, in fact.

Rosalie stood, walking across to the massive plate-glass window that overlooked half of Kensington. She stared into the street below without really seeing any of the little ant-type figures scurrying about, a frown wrinkling the pure line of her brow.

She could remember the exact moment she had walked into Jamie's large and very plush drawing room in Richmond and glanced across the assembled couples, only to find her gaze held and transfixed by a pair of piercingly blue eyes, which had narrowed to twin points of light on her face. She had been aware of David at the side of her saying something, but for the life of her she had been unable to move or speak. And then the cerulean gaze, its deep blue as clear as a summer's sky, had released her, the man in question turning his head in answer to something the woman on his arm had said. She had taken a deep and very necessary gasp of air, deep enough for David to say anxiously, 'Are you all right, Lee? What's the matter?'

'The matter? Nothing,' She forced a smile, before adding, 'How are you feeling? That's more to the point.' David was an old and very dear university friend who had just been through a painful and acrimonious divorce, which had caused him to totter on the edge of a nervous breakdown for months. The evening was his first venture into the social scene since his wife had left him, taking their two children to live with her new lover, and he had been visibly shaking in the taxi earlier. Only the fact that they were as comfortable together as a pair of old shoes had persuaded him to leave his recently acquired bachelor flat when she had called for him.

'I'm okay.' His smile was more of a grimace and Rosalie felt for him. 'It's just that I've never been much good at this sort of thing, dinner parties and such. Ann was always the one who was the life and soul of the party.'

Ann had been a cold-hearted, predatory exhibitionist who had systematically alienated every other female she had ever come into contact with, along with making a play for every man. However, Rosalie thought it wasn't the right time to point that out.

'Nonsense,' she said briskly. 'You're great company, you always have been, it's just that your confidence has taken a bit of a mauling lately.' Which was putting it mildly. 'Now, we're just going to circulate and smile and make polite conversation whilst we sip one of Jamie's magnificent cocktails and contemplate the superb dinner ahead. Did you know he's buttonholed one of the chefs from Hatfields tonight? Apparently he's a friend of a friend and Jamie's offered him a small fortune to come and put on this dinner on his evening off.'

'Really?' David was an accountant and now the pound sign showed in his eyes. 'How much is a small fortune?'

'Ask Gabby, she'll be sure to know.' Rosalie guided him over to one of their more inquisitive friends who had a reputation for winkling anything out of anyone, and stood listening with some amusement to their conversation.

That died abruptly when a smooth voice at her elbow

said, 'Rosalie. Unusual name. French origin, I think?' and she turned to see the possessor of the faint American burr.

Kingsley Ward was tall, very tall, with a muscled strength that made the beautifully tailored dinner jacket sit on him like a designer's dream, Rosalie remembered now, her cheeks flushing at the memory. He was hard and ruggedly handsome, his face one of sharply defined planes and angles, which said he took no prisoners, and she gazed up at him with a sensation akin to numbness freezing her response. Ebony hair cut very short along with ridiculously thick eyelashes emphasised the brilliant blue of his eyes even more close to, but it was the overall sense of maleness that was so intimidating. Uncomfortably, unsettlingly intimidating. Enough to make her want to turn tail and run.

Instead she lifted her chin ever so slightly, calling on all the resources of her thirty-one years as she said coolly, 'My mother was French.'

'That explains the chic and classical elegance.'

Yuk, what a smoothie! And if there was anything she disliked it was handsome smooth-talkers who thought they were God's gift to the female race.

She was unaware that her thoughts were mirrored in her eyes until the warm social smile and interested expression on the hard face vanished. His gaze took on the quality of blue ice, and he said coolly, 'I have obviously interrupted a riveting conversation you are anxious to get back to. Excuse me,' at which point he turned and walked away, leaving her feeling more than a little ashamed of herself. And she *hated* feeling like that.

The way the evening had gone thus far she supposed it was inevitable she was seated between David and Kingsley Ward for dinner. He was coldly polite to her, and charming and amusing to everyone else, and as she sat and listened to the banter as the meal progressed she was forced to admit he was excellent company.

But of course men like Kingsley Ward often *were* excellent company, Rosalie reminded herself now, turning from the window. They loved to be the centre of attention for one thing, and for another, with natural attributes like devastating good looks and a physique most men would kill for, they had a self-confidence and air of sexy wickedness that was an aphrodisiac all in itself.

Was *that* why she had dressed with such care this morning? And then she answered the nasty little probing voice from her conscience with a sharp, No, not at all! She always made sure she was well turned out for the office, and with a prospective new client it was extra important. That was all. That *definitely* was all.

The wrist-watch reminded her it was a minute to ten and bite-the-bullet time. She sat down again at her desk, smoothed her hair and took a deep breath. She resisted the impulse to check her make-up in the mirror in her cosmetics bag and felt quite proud of herself for doing so.

'Right.' She pressed the intercom. 'I can see Mr Ward now, Jenny,' she said brightly.

A moment or two later the door opened and Jenny all but curtsied Kingsley Ward into the room, Rosalie noticed with a dart of annoyance as her back stiffened for the onslaught of the piercingly blue gaze. But she was prepared for it this time. Her heart was thudding but outwardly she was the epitome of the successful businesswoman, cool, collected and *very* in control. 'Good morning, Mr Ward.' She had been determined to get the first word in and set the tone. 'Won't you sit down?'

She hadn't offered to shake his hand, which was something that would have been automatic usually, but—and she acknowledged it was stupid—she didn't want to touch him.

Kingsley Ward had no such inhibitions. He strode across the office, hand outstretched, as he responded, 'Good morning, Rosalie. I may call you Rosalie? And you must call me Kingsley, or King if you prefer.'

The last was said in just the same brisk voice as the rest of his opening gambit, but Rosalie had looked into his face and she was sure she saw something mocking there.

As her small hand was enfolded in a giant one that was warm and hard, she steeled herself to show no reaction at all. Nevertheless, her breathing wasn't quite even when she said, withdrawing her hand the very second it wasn't rude to do so, 'How may Carr and Partners help you?' as she gestured again for him to be seated.

She was a cool one all right, and just as sleek and sophisticated as he remembered from that damn awful dinner party. Kingsley folded himself into the seat opposite the desk, his long legs crossed one over the other and his arms going out along the arms of the upholstered chair in a pose that was naturally masculine. True, the elegant cocktail dress had been replaced by a beautifully tailored business suit, but the silver-blue shade brought out the copper tints in that wonderful chestnut hair and turned the grey eyes mother-of-pearl. He hadn't seen such a naturally lovely woman in years, so how come his careful enquiries had revealed there was no man in her life at present, nor had there been for some time as far as anyone knew? Of course she could just be an obsessive career woman married to her job, but... The soft mouth was too full and the small chin too vulnerable for that.

He smiled, slowly. 'We started off on the wrong foot

at Jamie's dinner party, didn't we?' he drawled easily. 'How about we try again?'

How about we don't? Rosalie lifted fine eyebrows in polite enquiry. 'I'm sorry, I don't quite understand?' she said frostily.

He stared at her for a moment, just long enough for her cheeks to begin to turn a definite pink, and then he shrugged, straightening in the chair and picking up the briefcase he had placed at the side of him when he had sat down. 'Ward Enterprises acquired just over a hundred acres of land situated between Oxford and London a few weeks ago,' he said curtly as he opened the briefcase and extracted some paperwork. 'I want to build a hotel and country club, with an eighteen-hole golf course, land-scaped gardens, helicopter landing pad and so on, similar to the ones I own in the States. Here is the architect's plan and the full brief. Interested?' He pushed the papers over the desk before settling back in his chair again.

Interested? Suddenly becoming aware that her mouth had fallen open in a small gape, Rosalie shut it with a little snap, her cheeks brilliant now. She had been so rude to him—*so rude*—and all the time there had been the possibility of this fabulous project for Carr and Partners. Why hadn't anyone at Jamie's told her that he was an entrepreneur—and a pretty wealthy one if this was any-thing to go by? But she had been looking after David for most of the evening, she reminded herself feverishly; that was when she hadn't been ignoring Kingsley Ward, of course.

'May I examine these for a moment?' Her voice sounded remarkably normal considering she felt about an inch tall.

'Sure, take all the time you want.'

Concentrate, Lee, concentrate. As she spread out the

plan and attempted to look at it it danced before her eyes for a second or two before she took a deep breath and willed her racing heart to behave. It didn't help that Kingsley Ward was straight in front of her with his gaze fixed on her face—she might not be looking at him now but she could feel those twin lasers on her skin.

After a little while professionalism took over and she became engrossed in the plan and brief, excitement growing like an expanding ball in her stomach. This was a terrific job and a fantastic opportunity, but she had to admit one of the other partners—*any* of the other partners—was more qualified for such a massive undertaking than she.

Mike, Peter and Ron were all well over forty. Mike was approaching fifty-five, with a wealth of experience to draw on, and she was very much the junior partner. She would have to make it clear to Kingsley Ward that if Carr and Partners were given the job, one of the other partners would almost certainly insist he took over.

She raised her head. He was sitting in the same pose as before, leaning back against the seat, breathtakingly relaxed and sure of himself, but this time the almost tangible authority brought no irritation, all her senses tied up with how best to put what she was going to say. 'Mr Ward—'

'Kingsley,' he interrupted, very softly.

She nodded, her cheeks—which had just cooled—firing up again. She had always loathed the way she blushed so easily but it went hand in hand with the red lights in her chestnut hair and there was nothing she could do about it. 'Kingsley,' she began again, 'this is a wonderful job and I know Carr and Partners would be thrilled to take it on if you saw fit to put it our way—'

'But?'

She had always taken exception to being interrupted, she considered it the height of rudeness, and now she breathed out just once before she continued, 'But I'm afraid you are talking to the wrong person. My partners are all older and more experienced, and they would be able to tackle this project far better than me, much as I would love to do it.'

He shifted slightly in the chair, lean male thighs outlined for a moment or two under the Armani suit, and Rosalie's nerves jerked. 'You would love to do it?' he said quietly.

'Yes, of course, but you would need someone who—'

'Then do it.' It was as though he hadn't heard her. She stared at him, and he said softly, 'Let me put it another way. I am not a fool, Rosalie, and I would not offer you the job if I did not think you were capable of doing it. I have been assured from various quarters that to date you have handled your work competently, ethically and thoroughly, and more than one person has told me that you are particularly skilful in detecting problems with builders before they occur. Am I right?'

She was pinned by the blue eyes and could do no more than nod her head.

'Good.' He spoke as if the matter was settled and Rosalie had a moment of panic.

She cleared her throat. 'The thing is, the decision is not up to me,' she said carefully.

'No, it is up to me,' he agreed shortly, standing. Rosalie rose quickly, her head spinning. Was he leaving already? It appeared so. 'Discuss the job with your partners, by all means, but make it clear I am engaging *you*, please. If they need to speak to me you have my number in England and in the States on the information I have given you.'

He was already walking to the door as he spoke and

then he paused, turning to look at her. 'Do you feel you could do the work, given the chance?' he asked quietly. 'You said you would love to do it but that isn't necessarily the same thing. The time angle is not so much of a problem, I can be flexible to a degree.'

She was still reeling with the suddenness of it all but there was no hesitation in her voice when she said, 'Yes, I can do it. I've not tackled anything on this scale before, I have to admit, but, yes. The job I'm working on at the moment will be finished within a week or so, and after that there is nothing planned which I can't pass on to one of the others.'

'Good.' It was silky soft. 'My secretary will liaise with you as necessary, but I am a hands-on kind of guy, Rosalie, so we'll be seeing quite a bit of each other over the next months.'

Rosalie blinked. The words sounded innocent enough but there had been a smoky flavour to them that had set her antennae waving. And then she told herself not to be so silly. This was work, business, that was all. Kingsley Ward was obviously an enormously successful and wealthy mogul, and with his looks, not to mention his money and male charisma, he must have the women lining up in droves. It had been one of the things that had set her teeth on edge at Jamie's wretched dinner party—the way every woman present had been all but dribbling with lust. And of course he'd lapped up the attention; what man wouldn't?

He was waiting for a response. She pulled herself together as the realisation hit, stitching a polite smile on her face with some effort. 'We've still got a way to go before you give Carr and Partners the work, surely?' she said evenly. 'You haven't asked the fee for my services.'

She realised too late she could have put that better when

the blue eyes flickered, just once, and he said, very dryly, 'What exactly do you charge, Rosalie?'

With anyone else she could have turned it into a joke or frozen the individual out with one of the icy looks she had perfected years ago, but Kingsley Ward wasn't anyone else. And she was burning up with enough heat to spontaneously combust.

Rosalie took the coward's way out and acted dumb. 'For a job of this kind we tend to estimate a cost,' she said tightly. 'It isn't always possible to be specific when one is dealing with contractors and subcontractors, and things don't always go according to plan. Materials might not be available when they ought to be, for example, or there may be a technical hitch which makes the job more difficult and therefore more time-consuming. Of course, this is not usually the case,' she added quickly.

'Quite,' he said soothingly, making her aware she was gabbling.

'The first thing I would need to do is to draw up a bill of quantities, which is a list of all the materials needed to complete the project right down to the smallest detail. This would extend to several hundred pages for a job of this nature.'

He held up a restraining hand, his voice even dryer when he said, 'You are telling me you don't come cheap, is that it?'

She had never met anyone she would like to punch on the nose more, or anyone who could make the most normal conversation sizzle with sexual undertones like this man. Or was it her? The thought kicked like a mule. Was she imagining all this? She didn't like being confused and it sounded in her voice when she said, 'It's always worth paying for the best in the long run.'

'My sentiments exactly,' he drawled silkily, his

American accent suddenly strong. 'And that being the case I am sure I will hear from you shortly with a tidy breakdown, and some sort of ceiling cost, okay?'

'Yes, of course.' He had opened the door before she realised she hadn't thanked him for what was the most fantastic opportunity of her career to date, but even as the words hovered on her tongue he had gone without a backward glance or a goodbye.

CHAPTER TWO

ROSALIE worked harder than she had ever done over the next few weeks. Once she'd finished with the job she'd been engaged on when Kingsley Ward had made his amazing proposition, she began working on the bill of quantities for the Ward project, which was an enormous undertaking. It didn't help that she was aware her three senior partners were a little anxious about it all.

When she had told Mike Carr and the other two about the meeting with Kingsley Ward, Mike had called Kingsley the same day, after which he had come and perched on her desk in the late evening just as Rosalie had been thinking of going home.

'There's no doubt he wants you for the job.' Mike looked at the slim, beautiful woman in front of him, whom he both respected and admired, and in whom he had taken a fatherly interest almost from the first day Rosalie had begun at Carr and Partners fresh from university ten years before. 'Know much about him, do you?'

Rosalie stared at him in surprise. Mike was more than a working colleague; shortly after she had been engaged by the firm she had discovered she had been at university with his daughter, Wendy, and after a reunion with the other girl it had become common for her to spend the odd weekend at the Carrs' lovely old house in Harrow. The family's friendship had come at a painful time in her private life and had meant the world. It still did, even though—with Wendy now married and living abroad, and Rosalie having been taken on as junior partner, which had

17

doubled her workload and made for less socialising—she saw less of the family as a whole.

'Not a thing, really,' she admitted after a moment or two. 'Why? Isn't he creditworthy?'

Mike smiled. 'You really don't know anything about him, do you? Oh, yes, he's creditworthy, all right, Lee. Ward Enterprises was begun by his father over thirty years ago, but until Kingsley was old enough to come on board it was just a moderately successful little hotel chain comprising of some three or four fairly middle-of-the-road establishments. Kingsley changed all that. He had the vision to buy up land and make the Ward name synonymous with luxury hotels complete with a couple of golf courses, hundreds of acres of parkland and so on, the sort of places the rich and famous would go to to enjoy peace and seclusion where their every need is catered for. To put it crudely, my dear, Kingsley Ward is loaded.'

Rosalie smiled, before raising her eyebrows as she said, 'So why that note in your voice when you asked me if I knew anything about him?'

'What note?' And then Mike smiled himself at the expression on his junior partner's face. 'Oh, all right,' he said a little shamefacedly. 'It's just that, along with the wealth and jet-set lifestyle the man now has, has come a certain reputation.'

Rosalie's eyebrows rose higher.

'He's partial to a well-turned ankle.'

Dear Mike. Only he could use such a quaint old-fashioned phrase to describe a womaniser, Rosalie thought fondly, before she said teasingly in a mock American accent, 'You mean he likes the broads?'

Mike wasn't smiling now. 'He likes them, all right,' he said quietly. 'Lots of them.'

'What's that got to do—?' Rosalie stopped abruptly.

'Oh, come on, Mike,' she said disbelievingly, 'you don't seriously think a man like the one you've just described would waste time trying to seduce a little provincial mouse like me, do you? He's used to the celebs and model types who have been everywhere and done everything for sure.'

'Rosalie, you're a very beautiful woman, and no one in his right mind would describe you as a mouse,' Mike said matter-of-factly. It was always amazing to him that she seemed so completely unaware of her effect on the opposite sex. What did she see when she looked in the mirror, for crying out loud? It was a question he'd asked himself many times, and now he answered it as he usually did; she saw something different from everyone else for certain. And she had Miles Stuart to thank for that. 'Anyway, all I'm saying is watch him, okay? I'd say the same to Wendy in a similar situation, you know that.'

'Yes, I know, Mike.' She put out a hand and touched his jacket sleeve. 'And I appreciate it, but, really, there's no need.'

Nevertheless, that conversation of a few weeks ago was now on Rosalie's mind as she finished the last item in the bill of quantities and settled back in her seat in front of the word processor. Kingsley had asked her to contact him once she had this ready and before she sent copies to various contractors to put a cost on each part of the work. She had got the impression he was the type of man who liked to keep his finger on even the tiniest pulse. She would try the English number he had given her first and ask his secretary where he was in the world. Since the conversation with Mike she had made it her business to find out everything she could about Kingsley Ward, and she had discovered he had hotels in the Caribbean as well as the States and was constantly on the move. She had also found out that Mike had not exaggerated about Kingsley's love life.

She dialled the number herself; she had come into the office very early to finish off the list of materials and, as it was now still only eight o'clock in the morning, Jenny hadn't arrived. Undoubtedly her call would be intercepted by an answer machine in Kingsley's new English office in Oxford, but that was all right. It was another thing off the multitude of jobs she'd got lined up for the day, and his secretary could call Jenny later.

'Kingsley Ward.'

Rosalie almost dropped the telephone at the sound of the deep cold male voice, her heart giving a resounding thump. It was a moment or two before she could say, 'K...Kingsley?' Oh, don't stutter, girl, for goodness' sake, she told herself in the next instant, hearing her breathless voice with utter contempt. Her voice was stronger as she continued, 'It's Rosalie Milburn here from Carr and Partners.'

There was a pause, and then, 'Yes, Rosalie?'

She gulped. She preferred the first abrupt cold voice to the warmer, faintly sexy burr with which he'd spoken her name. And then she told herself not to be so darn ridiculous and to get on with it. 'I'm sorry to bother you so early,' she said politely. 'I was expecting to just leave a message on your secretary's answer machine to say that the bill of quantities is ready that you wanted to look over, and to ask where to send it. I wasn't sure if you were in England or America.'

'That was quick,' he said appreciatively. 'I'm in London today, I'll call in for it. There were a couple of things I wanted to discuss with you anyway. Are you free for lunch?'

'L...Lunch?' She was doing it again! Her brain scrambled. She wasn't doing anything for lunch but the last thing she wanted was to spend a couple of hours in close proximity to Kingsley Ward with no hope of escape. And then logic and reason took over. This was a massive job, she was going to have to liaise with Kingsley considering he was the type of man who insisted on overseeing everything. She forced her voice into neutral. 'Lunch would be fine.'

'Great.' If he'd sensed her hesitation he gave no sign of it when he said, 'I'll pick you up round noon, okay?'

'Yes. Thank you.'

The phone went click. No goodbye, no social pleasantries. A man of few words, obviously. Rosalie sat staring at the receiver for some seconds, aware that she was feeling rail-roaded but that it wasn't really fair on Kingsley. She could have said no to lunch, but if he needed to talk to her there was no point, added to which she had to make herself get on enough with him for them to establish a working relationship.

She looked down at what she was wearing. She had dressed for an unremarkable day in the office—pencil-slim grey trousers and a wrapover white buttoned shirt, with a pearl-grey bouclé wool jacket for later in case the May evening turned chilly on the walk home. Her flat was only half a mile from the office and she always travelled on foot, enjoying the wake-up in the morning and the wind-down at night. The only time she drove was when she needed to call on site or visit an architect or contractor or something similar.

She wrinkled her nose at her clothes. Kingsley Ward would be used to women who dressed to kill, for sure. And then she caught the errant thought, horrified at herself. What did it matter what he was used to? This was a business lunch with a client, that was all. As long as she was presentable that was all that mattered, and Kingsley probably wouldn't notice what she was wearing anyway.

Kingsley did. He arrived to collect her just before noon, his gaze going over her steadily as Jenny ushered him into Rosalie's office. Rosalie made a huge effort to act as she would with a man who wasn't drop-dead gorgeous, smiling brightly and forcing herself to extend her hand this time as she said, 'Kingsley, how nice to see you again.'

His smile was lazy, with a mocking quality that suggested he knew she was lying. 'Likewise.'

'I've got everything ready if you'd like to glance through before we leave?' she asked briskly, once her flesh had left contact with his. The tingling in her hand she could do nothing about.

'Later. I'm hungry.' His gaze hadn't left her face, his eyes like blue crystal.

'Fine.' She busied herself in collecting the wool jacket and her handbag, hoping her bustle hid her agitation. She had forgotten what a startlingly deep blue his eyes were; if it were anyone else but Kingsley Ward she would have suspected they were wearing cosmetic contact lenses.

'I hope you had nothing pressing this afternoon? I would like to visit the site after lunch. The architect will be there and it would be good for you to meet him.'

'Of course.' Rosalie thought of her work schedule and prayed for calm. 'I'm all yours.'

The carved lips twitched. 'How generous.'

It was, actually. She had already visited the site twice and didn't really need to meet the architect today, Rosalie thought aggressively. There would be time enough for that once the tenders were returned, a builder selected and the work began. It would be her job to see the chosen builder kept to his prices, and she would be visiting the site frequently to value the work done for interim payments.

'Shall we?' He had taken her arm and whisked her out of the office before she had time to reflect further, and it was with dark amusement that Rosalie noticed Jenny's expression of envy. If her secretary had but known it she would have swopped places with her for the lunchtime like a shot!

Carr and Partners was situated in a row of terraced houses, and once out on the pavement Kingsley led the way to a nifty little silver sports car that would have done credit to James Bond. Rosalie was eternally grateful to her guardian angel that she'd decided to wear trousers that day; the car's low interior was not conducive to entering and exiting in anything else. As it was she slid into the leather interior with more than a measure of aplomb. This faded somewhat when Kingsley climbed into the driver's seat. He was close, very close, and he smelt nothing short of delicious.

Rosalie hit her traitorous libido a sharp crack on the knuckles and swallowed deeply a few times. Her voice higher pitched than usual, she said, 'Is it far? Where we're eating?'

Damn it, but she was like a cat on a hot tin roof. Was it him or was she like this with the whole male race? 'No, not far,' he said easily as he pulled out into the traffic, the car's engine growling softly. 'A friend of mine owns a little place near Finsbury Park where I often eat when I'm in London. Unless there's somewhere else you'd prefer?' He glanced at her.

She shook her head, making the silky swirl of hair move and shimmer. Kingsley felt his loins tighten in response and turned his head, concentrating on the traffic.

After a few tense moments during which Rosalie registered every single movement he made and the car's interior seemed to shrink still more, she said carefully, 'I'm really excited about this job, and I never did thank you for looking me up after the dinner party. Who mentioned I was a quantity surveyor, anyway?'

He executed a manoeuvre that was totally illegal, receiving a few kindly gestures from passing motorists in the process, before he said, 'What? Oh, I don't remember. Is it important?'

He turned to look behind him as he changed lanes and Rosalie glanced at the back of his head where his hair had been tapered into his neck. It was so sexy it wasn't true. As the big body turned again her head shot to the front. She felt like a voyeur, for goodness' sake, she admitted to herself crossly, willing each taut muscle to slowly relax. But she hadn't expected to be cocooned in an inch-square box with him, that was the thing.

Kingsley was clearly a man who didn't go in for chatter when he was driving, and the short journey was accomplished in almost total silence. By the time they drew up outside a small neat restaurant Rosalie felt she'd got her act together, in spite of not quite being able to identify what it was about Kingsley Ward that threw her into such a spin.

True, he was silver-screen handsome with the added authority that came with wealth and influence, but he was also hard, ruthless and possessed of a giant ego, from all the background she'd gathered on him. Women galore had been enjoyed and discarded if half the stories about him were true, and Rosalie didn't doubt that they were, looking at the man. And she loathed men like him, individuals who took and never gave, plundered and demanded what they wanted as though it were their God-given right. In fact they disgusted her.

'Don't you like it?'

'What?' She spun round in her seat as the quiet voice registered on her, becoming aware in that moment that her face must have reflected her thoughts as she gazed out unseeing at the building in front of them. 'Oh, I'm sorry, I was thinking of something else,' Rosalie said quickly. 'This looks very nice.'

'Don't let the nondescript appearance fool you,' he said evenly as he cut the engine. 'Glen isn't into glitz and glamour, but he has the punters fighting a path to his door now word has got out about the food here.'

He exited the car in a smooth, controlled uncurling motion that Rosalie could but envy; she knew she was going to have far more trouble levering herself out of the low seat. As it was he had opened her door and extended a hand before she had to try, and once she was standing on the pavement she tried to ignore his towering height and the fact that she was all flustered again.

Kingsley opened the door of the restaurant for her and then waved her through in front of him, thinking as he did so, Nice bottom. In fact nice everything. She was one hell of a woman and yet there was something so fiercely defensive about her it screamed disastrous love affair. Who had let her down and had it been recently? Certainly Jamie and one or two other of her friends who had been at the dinner party claimed they knew nothing. He wasn't sure if he believed them. Whatever, she intrigued him. She'd intrigued him that night, enough for him to follow through and arrange for her to get the quantity surveyor's job, after he had checked her credentials, of course. Much as he liked the idea of being the hunter for a change, he wasn't about to endanger what was a very tasty business opportunity because he wanted a woman who had made it clear she didn't want him.

'King! My friend, my friend.'

Rosalie hadn't expected the said Glen to be foreign, somehow—Glen sounded too English for that—but the slim, wiry man who came rushing up as they entered was Italian or she'd eat her hat. He kissed Kingsley on both cheeks—something Kingsley had obviously been expecting and which didn't phase him at all—before turning his attention to her, saying, 'You have brought the most beautiful lady in London to grace my restaurant. How can I thank you, my friend?'

'Cut the spiel, Glen,' Kingsley said dryly, 'it won't work on this lady. And she's a business colleague, before you get too carried away.'

'So there is hope for me? Even better!'

The black eyes were wicked but full of laughter, and Rosalie found herself laughing back as she said, 'If the food is as good as the welcome, no wonder you are so popular.'

'Rosalie; Glen Lorena, the biggest sweet-talker this side of the ocean. Glen; Rosalie Milburn, my new quantity surveyor for the English job.'

'This is true?' The Latin face expressed surprise. 'But you are too lovely to do such work. I cannot believe this.'

'Believe it, buddy.' Kingsley had noticed the dimming of Rosalie's smile and took swift action, ushering her further into the restaurant as he said over his shoulder, 'Usual table free?'

'Of course, my friend, of course. The moment I received your reservation the table became yours.'

Glen joined them a moment later, taking their order for drinks as he presented them with two dog-eared menus before disappearing again. Rosalie glanced round. The room was not large and it was packed with diners, in spite of the furniture being on the basic side without a taste of luxury anywhere. They were sitting in what was clearly a prime position in a small alcove, a table that gave an element of privacy without obstructing the view.

As her eyes returned to Kingsley he leant forward slightly. 'Glen didn't mean anything by that last remark,' he said softly. 'It's just his way. His wife used to work as a barrister before they got this place so he's got no problem with women and careers.'

Rosalie nodded stiffly. It was true she hadn't appreciated the Italian's comment about her job; she'd suffered the same sort of surprise too often in the past, normally accompanied by a distinctly patronising interest afterwards. After a degree course followed by three years of practical training and then the Assessment of Professional Competence, she felt she'd served a good apprenticeship before she began working as a fully qualified surveyor in what was still very much a male-dominated environment.

She had found she had to be just that bit better than her male colleagues at first to be taken seriously, but being a female in such a position was definitely a situation of swings and roundabouts. Most of the builders were tickled pink to see her arrive on site, and, once they realised she knew her onions and wasn't going to be fooled or cajoled into accepting late dates or poor quality work, they were pussy-cats in her hands.

She'd often heard Mike and the others bemoaning the fact that they got all the stick from both the builder's own surveyors and also the client when things went wrong, but usually, with just a smidgen of charm, her jobs ran on nicely oiled wheels.

'Whilst we're on the subject of careers,' Kingsley continued smoothly, 'what *did* make you take up quantity surveying?'

Rosalie stared at him. She hadn't been aware they were

on the subject of anything. She shrugged after a moment or two, her lashes sweeping down and hiding her gaze from the piercing one opposite as she said carefully, 'I liked the mix of office work and getting my hands dirty on site, I suppose.'

'Commerce is a hard world,' Kingsley said quietly, 'especially for a woman dealing with men who might not like being told what to do or not to do by a female, and a young and attractive one at that.'

Rosalie shrugged again. 'I'm tougher than I look,' she said without smiling.

He gazed at her, one dark eyebrow quirked and a disturbing gleam in the back of the brilliant eyes. 'Are you now?' he murmured softly. 'A lady of mystery?'

'There's no mystery.' She had spoken too quickly and she knew it as well as he did. She buried her face in the menu.

So, he'd hit a nerve? Kingsley's eyes narrowed a fraction as he sat back in his seat just as one of the waiters arrived with the bottle of wine and another of sparkling mineral water. Life had taught him a few lessons in his thirty-five years on the earth, he reflected as he watched the waiter filling their glasses. One, expensive wine was worth every dollar compared to the other stuff. Two, gambling was a mug's game. Three, never trust a woman, especially a beautiful one with hair like bronzed silk and eyes the colour of a stormy sky, eyes that carried secrets in their cloudy depths. For sure the secrets would be nothing more important than what hair dye she used to colour her hair, and within a few weeks he would be itching to move on. Although Rosalie's hair looked natural...

He picked up the menu, suddenly annoyed with his thoughts and the world in general although he couldn't have explained why. 'The roasted shallot and lemon thyme salad is very good to start with,' he suggested mildly. 'One of Glen's specialities. Or the mediterranean fish soup? And I can recommend the roast lamb or braised tangerine beef with herb dumplings.'

Rosalie smiled politely. She chose watercress soufflé followed by poached fillet of sea bass with asparagus tips, and after she had given her order to Glen, who had reappeared like the proverbial genie out of a bottle, she sat back in her seat and had a couple of hefty swallows of the very good wine whilst she watched Kingsley discussing the merits of the lamb against the beef with his friend. If ever she had needed a drink it was now, she thought with wry self-mockery. Why ever she had agreed to come out to lunch with this disturbing individual she didn't know, let alone commit to spending what virtually amounted to a whole afternoon in his presence.

When the food came it was utterly delicious, although Rosalie had to admit that Kingsley's Mediterranean fish soup and roast lamb looked and smelt wonderful, added to which she had never particularly cared for sea bass. But her food was excellent, all of it, along with the wine and the chocolate macadamia steamed pudding drenched with whipped cream she chose for dessert. She didn't think she had ever tasted food so good, and she told Kingsley so as they drank their coffee.

He smiled. He'd smiled quite often during the meal as they had made light conversation, and she had to concede he'd got the art of conversation, along with the smile, down to a T. But the smile had never reached the cool blue of his eyes and the conversation was such that she knew nothing more about him than when they had first sat down at the table. Which was enough, more than enough, she told herself dryly.

'Glen's easily the best chef I've ever come across.'

Kingsley drained his coffee-cup and gestured to the hovering waiter for the bill. 'As the waiting list for a table bears out.'

'Surely he could earn a fortune if he chose to work somewhere like the Savoy or the Ritz?' Rosalie asked, her eyes wandering round the interior of the restaurant again.

'He's done the big-time thing and ended up nearly ruining his marriage *and* his health,' Kingsley said shortly. 'He got out of the rat race, bought this place and set up with Lucia, his wife, who does all the behind-the-scenes work. He's had offers galore to go back as a head chef or expand here to bigger and better, but the bottom line is he doesn't need it. He's happy here, Lucia's happy, that's all that matters to Glen in the long run. He's found his Shangri-La.'

Rosalie stared at him. 'You sound as if you envy him,' she said at last.

He smiled but this time it didn't even crinkle the skin around his eyes. 'Why would I do that?' he said easily. 'I'm exactly where I want to be in life. How about you?'

'Me?'

'Yes, you. Are you where you want to be in life?' he asked with a silkiness Rosalie immediately suspected. 'Doing what you want, being who you want, with whom you want?'

She didn't like this conversation. 'Certainly,' she said briskly.

'Then we are both very fortunate.'

Rosalie's jaw set. She couldn't quite put a label on the quality of his voice but it suggested disbelief, and who the hell was Kingsley Ward to question her, anyway? 'Yes, we are.' She rose from her seat. 'I won't be a moment,' she said coolly before making her way to the door marked 'Signorinas' at the back of the restaurant.

Once in the small but immaculately clean little cloakroom Rosalie walked across to the two tiny washbasins situated under the plain, unframed mirror. She stared at the flushed reflection and two angry eyes stared back at her. She had done what she'd promised herself she wouldn't do weeks ago when she'd taken the job, and let Kingsley Ward get under her skin. Her soft lips tightened but her irritation was at herself and not Kingsley.

Self-control. It was all about self-control, everything was, she knew that. If *anyone* knew that, she did. She shut her eyes, shaking her head as it drooped forward, but today the memories she usually kept firmly under lock and key surfaced in a flood. Suddenly she was a little girl again, sitting shivering on the landing with her eyes straining down into the shadowed hall as she listened to the familiar sound of her father shouting at her mother in the sitting room below. Other sounds followed, they always did, but what made this occasion more memorable than all the ones that had gone before was that in the midst of the sound of slaps there came a silence, and then her father's voice, the tone agitated, saying, 'Chantal? Chantal, get up. Come on, get up.'

The memory blurred at this point but she could recall the bright lights of the ambulance and then the police car when they had arrived at the house. It had been a policewoman who had come and found her, still sitting in numb silence on the stairs. They had taken her to her maternal grandparents—her father had been brought up in a children's home and had no family—and it had been a day or two later when her grandmother had told her, very gently but with tears streaming down her face, that Mummy had gone to see the angels in heaven. Her beautiful, tender mother, who wouldn't have hurt a fly, had never recovered consciousness from the aneurysm that had begun to bleed in her head, caused by one of her husband's blows.

On the day of the court appearance her father had taken his own life, and at the age of five she had become an orphan. Her grandparents had looked after her from that point, and with her mother having had younger siblings who had gone on to have children her childhood had not been an unhappy one. But there had been a void, a massive gap because she had been a mummy's girl from the moment she had been born. As she had grown she had begun to understand why her mother had absorbed herself so completely in her child. Her grandparents had told her that her father had been an unhappy individual as a result of a traumatic childhood, insanely jealous of any attention his wife had paid to another adult, be they man or woman, and consequently her mother had led a life isolated from the rest of the world in an effort to keep the peace. Her headstone was a memorial that this hadn't worked.

Rosalie raised her head, her eyes large and dark with the painful memories. When she'd been eighteen and entering university her grandparents had decided to return to their native France to live their autumn years with the relatives there; her grandfather's health had been poor and he'd wanted to be close to his brothers.

She had agonised for some time whether to give up her university place in London and go with them, but she had been born in England and she didn't want to study in France, besides which there were all the friends she would leave behind. In the end she had stayed, and then she had met Miles Stuart...

'Enough.' She spoke the word out loud, her mouth setting in a grim line as she ruthlessly put a check on her mind. Why was she thinking of all this today? But she knew why. Miles and Kingsley Ward were miles apart in many ways, but they both had one attribute that was unmistakable: male magnetism.

It was indefinable, something elusive and subtle, but when a man had it, it cut through all the layers of civilisation and refinement and brought a woman right back to grass-roots level, forcing her to acknowledge a sexual response whether she wanted to or not. A powerful weapon. Her eyes darkened still more. And unfortunately mother nature seemed to excel in bestowing it on two-legged rats who didn't give a damn.

She breathed deeply before washing her hands, taking a moment or two to run her comb through her hair and apply fresh lipstick before she left the cloakroom and walked to where Kingsley was waiting near the front door of the restaurant. Glen was standing talking to him, and Rosalie kept her eyes on the Italian man as she said pleasantly, 'That was the best meal I've had in a long time, Glen.'

'It is a pleasure to cook for such a beautiful woman.' He grinned at her as he spoke, and Rosalie had to laugh. He was outrageous but somehow you knew he was as harmless as a kitten.

She turned her gaze to the long, lean figure beside the restaurateur, and eyes of blue ice looked back at her. 'All ready?' Kingsley asked easily, smiling the arctic smile.

Once out on the pavement in the fresh May sunshine, Rosalie remembered her manners. 'That was a lovely lunch,' she said politely. 'Thank you.'

'The pleasure was all mine.' An ordinary phrase, but he managed to make it sound like a criticism, as though she'd been churlish. She glanced at him and the azure eyes gazed back innocently.

This was going to be one great afternoon!

CHAPTER THREE

ROSALIE asked herself a hundred times afterwards how it had happened. Over the last ten years she had been to umpteen sites, clambering about measuring foundations and walls and areas of land, and not one accident. So why, *why* had it been this particular day at this particular site and more especially with this particular man that she'd had to go and make the most almighty fool of herself? One minute she had been talking to the architect and hopefully impressing Kingsley with her handle on the job, the next she'd been flat on her face with her ankle feeling as though it was broken.

The architect, a nice middle-aged man, was all concern, but it was Kingsley who picked her up in his arms after she had tried to rise and nearly passed out with the pain.

'I...I'm all right. Please, I can walk.' Through the excruciating throbbing the fact that she was being held close to a hard male chest with her head on an eyeline with his throat took precedence.

'Keep still.' She had tried to wriggle free and his voice was curt.

'Really, it feels better already,' she lied through gritted teeth.

'And I'm Mickey Mouse.'

The architect, who was now trotting alongside them as Kingsley carried her over to the parked cars, said soothingly, 'It might just be a sprain, Miss Milburn, but you really should get it checked at a hospital.'

'I'm not going to a hospital,' she responded quickly. 'Not for a sprain.'

'That's exactly where you're going,' the deep voice just above her head said flatly.

She would have argued better if she weren't so horribly conscious of being in his arms, but, with the feel of his body as he moved and the overall heady scent of faint whiffs of the most delicious aftershave, she wasn't feeling herself. 'If you'll just take me back to the office I will be fine,' she said as firmly as her twanging nerves would allow.

They had just reached the car and he didn't reply. As the architect opened the passenger door Kingsley placed her into the seat as carefully as one would a piece of Dresden china, but even so the action caused an involuntary gasp before she bit her lip hard, her face white.

'And you're talking about going straight back to the office?' he said disgustedly. 'Your ankle's already twice its size and swelling as we speak, or hadn't you noticed?'

Yes, she had darn well noticed; she was the one feeling the pain, not him!

He shut the passenger door, said a brief word to the architect who was now standing peering worriedly into the car, and then proceeded to make a call on his mobile phone. Rosalie was sure it was about her although she couldn't hear what was being said. He slid into the car, saying shortly, 'I'm taking you to a doctor.'

The man was like a cruise missile, but suddenly, what with the pain and the nausea it was causing, she couldn't argue anymore. Her face must have spoken for itself because he swore softly before reaching into the glove compartment and pulling out a small silver hip-flask, unscrewing the top and handing it to her. 'Drink some, it's brandy.'

'Brandy? I don't want—'

'*Drink some.*'

She drank, just a sip or two but she had to admit the neat alcohol burnt up the nausea causing her to feel more herself. And then she froze as Kingsley took off his jacket, bundling it into a roll and leaning over her as he said, 'I'm going to put this under your foot to cushion it as best we can, but I'm afraid the journey's not going to be pleasant.'

And then his head was practically in her lap as he positioned the clump of material that had been a very nice Armani jacket under the injured foot, easing off her court shoe as he did so.

She looked down at the short, spiky jet-black hair and muscled shoulders, and almost asked for another swig of brandy.

'Thank you.' She hoped he would put her breathlessness down to pain and ignore the flush of embarrassment that had flooded her cheeks with colour. He had only taken off his jacket, for goodness' sake, so why did it suddenly feel as if he were almost naked?

He eased himself back into the driving seat, loosening his tie and letting it hang slackly as he undid the first couple of buttons on his shirt.

He had a magnificent body. Her eyes just couldn't tear themselves away from the broad chest under the silk of his shirt. Powerful and lean, without an ounce of fat anywhere. She gave up trying to be cool and reached for the hip-flask again, taking another sip gratefully.

'Okay?' The blue eyes met hers, his voice low with sympathy now, and she gave a brave smile, nodding because she didn't trust her voice. Suddenly the hospital didn't seem such a bad idea—anything to get out of the claustrophobic confines of this car.

Having experienced Kingsley's driving technique earlier in the day, Rosalie appreciated he was driving extremely cautiously once they were underway, but nevertheless every slight jolt or bump of the car had her biting on her lip to stifle the gasps of pain.

She was conscious of him glancing at her a few times before they reached their destination, which looked to be a hospital nearer Oxford than London. As they drove into tree-filled grounds and she saw the long, modern attractive building in front of them she said, 'This isn't a private hospital, is it?'

'What's wrong with that?'

She hadn't got private health insurance, for a start.

Whether he guessed what she was thinking he didn't say, but what he did say was, 'This is where a friend of mine works and, as luck would have it, he's around today. He said he'd take a look at the ankle as a favour, and we'll go from there. Okay?'

This whole thing was running away from her and she didn't like that, besides which Kingsley seemed to have a friend for every occasion, Rosalie thought resentfully. It might be nasty of her in the circumstances when he was being so helpful, but she couldn't help the way she felt— he brought out the worst in her. She sat stiffly in her seat, her cheeks flaming. 'I would have preferred to go to a National Health hospital,' she said primly.

'Tough.' Her eyes shot to meet his at the tone, widening as he went on, 'I haven't got time to waste sitting in an emergency department even if you have. I have another appointment later.'

She glared at him. 'Well, excuse me!'

'Certainly.' The carved lips twitched at her fury. 'Now sit still until I can help you.'

Much as she hated to obey him she had no option, and

unfortunately she knew she was not going to be able to walk on the ankle either. Even trying to flex her toes brought acute agony. But the thought of him carrying her again... Could she hop, perhaps? Darn it, she'd never felt so helpless in all her life.

When he opened the passenger door the decision was taken out of her hands. He scooped her up before she could so much as utter a squeak. The warm masculine feel of his body was worse this time with just the silk of his shirt covering his chest.

'Put your arm round my neck,' he said quietly as he hotched her more securely against him. 'Don't worry, I don't bite.'

She was startled into looking up into his face; there had been a smoky quality to his voice that was pure dynamite. There had been wry amusement in his face at first, but then as their eyes locked she watched the amusement replaced by something else and found she was holding her breath, not daring to move a muscle.

Another car entering the car park broke the spell. Rosalie lowered her head, grateful for the wings of hair that covered her hot face, but by the time they walked into the reception of the hospital the burning colour had subsided due mainly to the ache in her foot.

The next half an hour was a painful one, and at the end of it Rosalie could have cried with frustration when X-rays confirmed Kingsley's friend's prognosis that a small bone was broken, necessitating a plaster cast on her ankle for a few weeks.

Another hour or so and they were back in the car again, the ankle feeling better now it was supported but Rosalie's head spinning as her brain scrambled all the appointments and deadlines of the next days. Fortunately a great deal of the work could be done from the office, she decided thankfully after a few minutes of thinking hard, and site visits would have to be undertaken by one of the others until she could drive again, unless she called on taxis. She would manage somehow, anyway. There was no way she was going to hand this job over, lock, stock and barrel, to someone else.

'How does it feel?'

'I'm sorry?' As Kingsley's voice penetrated her whirling thoughts Rosalie turned to him. She had to admit, albeit reluctantly, that he had been very good over this whole affair—refusing to let her pay for anything although she knew he had written a cheque at the hospital, and displaying a patience she hadn't suspected he possessed.

'The ankle. How is it?' he repeated, the patience she had noticed not so much in evidence now.

'Fine.' His irritation reminded her he'd had an appointment. 'I hope I haven't delayed you too long,' she added politely. 'You mentioned an appointment?'

'A dinner engagement.'

With a woman, she dared bet, and obviously one he was anxious to see if he was prepared to pay the expenses of a private hospital to keep his date. A dart of something Rosalie didn't care to put a name to made itself felt, causing her to silently upbraid herself. A man like Kingsley Ward would have any number of women, for goodness' sake, and gorgeous ones at that, but his private life was absolutely nothing to do with her.

She slanted a sideways glance at him from under her eyelashes. She had got used to the muscled contours of his body now—she'd had a couple of hours to do that at the hospital as he had insisted on staying with her—but still something warm curled in her stomach as she took in the hard profile and clean-cut lines. He was intensely sexy, she thought drowsily, the combination of the trauma of the accident and the pain-killers Kingsley's doctor friend had prescribed making her sleepy in the car's warm womb. She yawned before she could stop herself.

'Put your seat back and have a snooze,' Kingsley suggested a moment later, even though she hadn't been aware he had noticed.

For some reason the thought of being asleep and in a position where Kingsley could look at her and she wouldn't know was quite untenable. It woke her up better than a bucketful of cold water. 'No, it's okay,' she said quickly, adding, perfectly truthfully, 'I wouldn't sleep tonight if I had a nap now. I don't sleep well as it is.'

'No?' One rapier-sharp glance raked her face before returning to the road ahead. 'Why is that? Have you always been that way?'

Since Miles she had. Rosalie kept her voice even as she said, 'In latter years. It's not exactly unusual, after all.'

'First sign of stress.'

Rosalie stiffened at the hint of criticism. 'I don't think so. I enjoy my work,' she said very stiffly, eyes to the front.

'It doesn't have to be work that's the problem,' he countered smoothly. 'Work's not the be-all and end-all of life, surely.'

'The rest of my life is also perfectly stress-free, thank you,' she said tartly. As if it were anything to do with him, anyway.

'Rosalie, in this day and age *no one's* life is perfectly stress-free. Do you keep a healthy balance between work and play?' he persisted, knowing he was being unfair in pursuing this when she had just been through one hell of an afternoon, but sensing her defences were low. He wanted to know more about this woman who kept herself so very much to herself, he admitted silently, capitulating to the truth he had been ignoring all day. She had aroused his curiosity as well as his body, damn it, and, yes—it *was* pique he was feeling at her total disinterest in him. Which made him a lesser man than he had thought he was.

'That's my business, surely?' It was frosty, and exactly what he had expected.

'I'm sorry,' he said with lazy innocence. 'I've obviously touched a nerve.'

She glared at him. 'Of course you haven't,' she said sharply. 'That's absolutely ridiculous.'

The black eyebrows rose but he said nothing, which was ten times more aggravating than an argument, Rosalie thought irritably. It was hard to argue with silence.

'I mean it,' she said again. 'You haven't touched a nerve.'

'Methinks the lady protests too much.'

Methinks the gentleman is an arrogant pig.

'So, do you have a current partner, a boyfriend?' he asked softly, knowing the answer full well.

She was longing to tell him to mind his own business but in view of their conversation to date didn't think it appropriate. 'No.' It was so wintry ice tinkled.

It would have discouraged a lesser man, but Kingsley wasn't a lesser man. 'How long since you've been on a date, then?'

She was fairly quivering with the rage she was trying to hide. How dared he cross-examine her like this? 'In spite of this being the twenty-first century and therefore licence for most people to behave like rabbits, I prefer quality rather than quantity,' she responded icily, hoping that would be enough to satisfy him. She had never met such rudeness in her life.

Of course it wasn't. 'That taken as read, how long?'

Suddenly, horrifyingly, the rage had gone and the urge to burst into tears was paramount. Twelve years long. Twelve years since I was hurt and abused and brought to the brink of losing my mind. The words were so fierce in her head that for an awful moment she thought she'd spoken them out loud, but when the chiselled features didn't change she knew she was safe. She had never spoken about her relationship with Miles to anyone, not even her grandparents before they had died, and she never would. All old friends and family knew was that she'd been married and then it had finished. New friends didn't even know that much.

She took a deep pull of air, praying her voice wouldn't reveal her inward trembling. 'Some time, I can't remember. I'm not the sort of person who puts notches on the bedpost, unlike some.' She turned to look at him as she spoke.

It was pointed, and she saw his mouth tighten with a dart of gratification. You can dish it out but taking it is a little harder, isn't it? she thought bitterly.

'Meaning I am?' he asked grimly.

'I didn't say that.' She paused purposely. 'But if the cap fits…'

'It doesn't, not in this instance.'

'Right.' She put a wealth of meaning into the one word.

'I have my faults, Rosalie, but promiscuity is not one of them,' he said, very coldly.

'Methinks the gentleman protests too much.'

For a second she wondered if she had gone too far as she cast a sidelong glance at his angry face, and then the wind was completely taken out of her sails when he laughed ruefully, turning to look at her for an instant with eyes that were smiling for the first time since she had known him. *'Touché, mademoiselle,'* he said dryly. 'I guess I asked for that one.'

Oh, no, don't do this. Her mind was gabbling. Don't step out of the mould like this. You aren't the type who can laugh at himself. You're arrogant and self-opinionated and a control freak. It's written all over you in great big black letters.

'So…' It was a lazy drawl. 'You've got me down as a philanderer, is that it?' He glanced at her again.

She hesitated a mite too long.

'Charming.' It was dry but not too bothered.

'Look, Kingsley, I didn't exactly say that,' she said quickly as she reminded herself he *was* the best client Carr and Partners had had in ages. 'I don't know you, do I?'

'True.' They had just paused at some traffic lights and he turned to watch her with narrowed eyes. 'So how do we remedy that so you can give an informed opinion?'

'My opinion doesn't matter one way or the other, surely?'

His eyes travelled to her mouth, the fullness of the lower lip naturally pink and tender, and his voice was deep when he said, 'Perhaps I object to being misunderstood?' as he smiled again, sexily.

He was flirting with her. Rosalie stared at him for a moment and then the traffic lights changed to green and they were away. Whenever anyone had tried that in the past she had firmly repelled them, dealing with them gently or harshly depending first on their martial status, and then the nature of their persistence. Some of the married ones had been the worst, necessitating arctic freezing of the most severe magnitude, but there had been the odd young buck who had fancied his chances—along with his own sexual attraction—who had needed an icy put-down.

She hadn't found it difficult to deal with them, whatever

their age or experience, mainly—she realised right at this moment for the first time—because she hadn't been tempted by their overtures.

Kingsley was different. She gazed blindly ahead as the car growled and leapt forward. Which made him dangerous and to be avoided at all costs. She had done the falling-madly-in-love thing and it was a con; a repeat performance would make her the biggest fool on earth. Unfortunately, however, she had learnt over the last ten years that she wasn't the type to go in for sex without love; it just wasn't in her make-up. Therefore she'd decided a first-class career, and all the benefits that would accrue from it, was her goal in life.

Good friends, a nice home, enough money to travel to foreign parts when the fancy took her—that would suit her just fine. But the main thing, the most important thing, which transcended anything else and negated all other considerations and benefits, was that she remained autonomous. In control, with a capital C.

'I need an address.'

'What?' She came out of the maelstrom of her thoughts as his voice penetrated the turmoil.

'A finite end to the journey?' Kingsley could see her face even when he was concentrating on the road ahead, and he'd noticed the tight set to her mouth. He had known from the first moment he'd laid eyes on her at that damn dinner party that she spelt trouble, he told himself moodily. It was in the touch-me-not restraint of the slim, elegant body, the wary coolness in those magnificent eyes.

'If you could drop me at the office, I'll be fine.'

And who in hell had grey eyes anyway? He acknowledged her voice with irritation. Why not brown or blue or green? Those colours were good enough for most of the population, so why not Rosalie Milburn? 'I'll take you home.' It was a statement that did not invite argument.

'There's things I need to do.'

'Perhaps, but they'll keep till tomorrow. Those pain-killers are not to be messed with,' he said evenly. Why had she hovered on his consciousness from that first evening? He wasn't short of female company—the thought carried no pleasure, merely irritation—so what made this woman different? But then she wasn't, not really. She just played the game differently, that was all. Nevertheless, she stirred his blood until he couldn't think straight.

He ran his hand through his hair, more than a little annoyed with himself. He was too realistic and too cynical to pretend he believed in anything other than animal attraction between the sexes, he reassured himself in the next moment, but this woman had the plus factor in a way he hadn't come across in a long, long time. Which made it more strange she wasn't with anyone.

On the perimeter of his vision he saw Rosalie shift her injured foot, wincing as she did so, and the action emphasised to him how stubborn she was in asking to be taken to the office. She needed a hot meal and some more pain-killers and sleep, in that order, he thought flatly. Crazy woman.

'So, do I get an address or do we just drive round London all night?' His thoughts had made his voice abrupt, for which he offered no apology. She rattled him, he admitted it.

Rosalie glanced at him, her nostrils flaring at the tone. 'I live quite close to the office in Kensington,' she said shortly. 'I'll direct you when we get nearer.'

'Thank you.' It was sarcastic.

'You're welcome.' Why did he have to make everything into a confrontation?

The rest of the journey was conducted in silence until they reached Kensington, whereupon Rosalie duly directed him to the crowded terraced street where she lived. Number twenty was identical to its neighbours, and as Kingsley drew up outside the house he glanced at the five steps leading from the pavement to the front door. His expression said it all.

'I know; not ideal in the present circumstances,' Rosalie acknowledged tightly. But then she hadn't rented the flat with the possibility of becoming injured in mind. 'I'll get Jenny to bring some crutches round tomorrow,' she added, to let him know she wasn't totally oblivious to what was needed. 'That way I can be mobile again.'

'Mobile in the very loosest sense, I take it,' Kingsley qualified coolly, opening his door as he spoke.

As the tall lean figure exited the car Rosalie did something she hadn't done since childhood, and stuck out her tongue at the departing back. Okay, childish maybe, she thought guiltily, but he made her so mad she could spit.

When he opened the passenger door he didn't swoop on her immediately, letting his eyes wander over her face for a moment before he said, 'Do you often regress to kindergarten?'

The man must have eyes in the back of his head. Rosalie refused to blush this time. 'You deserved it,' she said stiffly. 'I'm trying to make the best of what is going to be a difficult and awkward situation for me, and your comment wasn't exactly helpful.' She glared at him, her mouth set tightly.

He considered, head slightly on one side. 'You're right. I apologise.' It was said with what sounded like genuine remorse.

She blinked. 'Yes, well, I should think so,' she said lamely. She didn't know what else to say.

'I'm glad you've accepted my apology so graciously.' He had gathered her up as he spoke and Rosalie was immensely pleased she'd had the foresight to get her key ready. He held her as she opened the door and then stepped with her into the wide hall. The house was three storeys high with a flat on each floor and a basement that housed the landlady of the property, and as Kingsley glanced about him and then looked towards the stairs, his voice was resigned when he said, 'Don't tell me, you live on the top floor?'

'This one actually,' she said smugly. 'That's my front door just there.' It felt enormously good to put him right.

He glanced down at her, his lips twitching at the satisfaction in her voice. 'Clever you,' he said softly, his eyes so blue they seemed luminous. His gaze intensified as it had done once before, but this time they were not in a car park and there were no interruptions.

Slowly his head bent and Rosalie made no move to avoid his mouth, watching with fascinated eyes as it came nearer. His lips were warm and firm as they touched hers in a fleeting kiss that held no threat, lingering just for an infinitesimal moment before he straightened, saying, 'Let's get you inside, you've had one hell of a day.'

He took the two or three steps to the white-painted front door before she had time to collect her scattered wits, and then she realised she was still holding the main front door key rather than the one to the flat. Her cheeks flushed, she found the appropriate key on her bulky keyring, which housed numerous office keys as well as personal ones, aware her hands were shaking and praying all the time he wouldn't notice.

She had allowed him to kiss her. Was she mad? She had to be! What on earth was he thinking now? Did he imagine it was an invitation for more of the same? Over her dead body!

She pushed the key into the lock, turned it, and then they were in her small square hall. 'I'll be fine now.' She tried to straighten but he took no notice of her efforts to be free, even when she said, 'Could you put me down, please?'

'Sitting room?' It was cool and unconcerned.

'What?' And then she collected herself, pointing to the first door off the hall as she said quickly, 'In there, but really you don't have to stay now. I know you have an appointment and it was good of you to bring me home.'

'This is great.' Once they were in the sitting room he glanced about him appreciatively, but Rosalie was in no mood to admire the décor, even if she had spent months decorating and furnishing her flat so it was exactly how she had imagined it on the morning she had first viewed it some years before.

The sitting room was the largest room with big windows that ensured there was lots of natural light, and she had made the most of this with a colour scheme of soft yellows and buttery cream, and pine furniture. She pointed now to the huge pine sofa that took up most of the far wall, and which was brimming with scattered cushions in varying shades. 'If you put me down there, I'll be fine,' she said again, making sure she kept her head bent so he couldn't possibly think she was propositioning him.

'I'm not going to leap on you, Rosalie.'

He put her down as requested as he spoke, gently and with care, and for a ridiculous moment she felt a sense of loss as the close contact finished before his words shocked her into raising her head. 'I know you aren't,' she lied vehemently. 'But you have a dinner engagement.'

'Did have,' he drawled, watching her with narrowed

eyes as he stepped back, crossing his arms. 'When Kirk was sure something was broken I cancelled it.'

'You shouldn't have done that,' she protested shakily.

He shrugged. 'Perhaps postponed is a better word. Does that make you feel better?' He didn't try to hide the mockery.

'But I'm—'

'Don't say fine.' He raised a hand, palm facing her. 'I couldn't stand it. Look, what sort of a guy do you think I am? You're in pain and the least I can do is to make sure you have something to eat before you turn in. Okay? Where's the kitchen?'

This was crazy. Her lips were still tingling from the brief contact with his and she wanted to ask him why he had kissed her, but the fact that he had seemed to dismiss it as totally unimportant made it difficult. In fact, if it weren't for the tingling she'd have wondered if she'd imagined it. But he *had* kissed her, and that wasn't in the contract. No way, no how. But how did you throw a six-foot-plus-a-few-inches, hard, lean, muscled man out of your flat when you couldn't even walk properly?

Her heart was beating so hard it hurt, but she managed to keep her voice very matter-of-fact when she said, 'I am more than capable of making myself a sandwich and after that lovely lunch I couldn't eat anything more.' That was a lie. She was amazed to find she was starving. Perhaps breaking a bone in your ankle was an appetite enhancer? Or perhaps it was all the nervous energy she expended around this man?

'A sandwich?' He eyed her reprovingly. 'It's—' he consulted the magnificent gold watch on his wrist '—now nearly eight, and we ate at one. You need something more than a sandwich and so do I.' It was a definite statement of fact, which brooked no reply.

It seemed churlish to tell him he was perfectly welcome to leave and go for a meal somewhere—considering he'd just told her he'd cancelled his dinner engagement for her—but that was exactly what she felt like doing. Rosalie bit back the words, saying instead, 'I'm afraid I don't have anything in. I was going to shop tonight on my way home.'

'Freezer food?' he suggested easily.

'Don't have one.' She tried to keep the triumph out of her voice. 'Cooking for one doesn't necessitate a freezer, besides which I prefer fresh produce.' So goodbye, Mr Know It All.

He smiled. 'That's okay, I was going to order some food in. Chinese, Indian, Italian, Thai?'

Rosalie gave up. Her ankle was too sore and she was too tired to argue any more. 'Chinese.'

He beamed. 'My favourite. Anything in particular you fancy?'

'Surprise me,' she said testily.

'Nothing I'd like better.' One dark eyebrow arched. 'Got a menu handy anywhere?'

'No, sorry.' She wasn't trying to be difficult, she genuinely *hadn't* got a menu. 'But there's an excellent Chinese take-away on the corner of the next street.'

He nodded, before walking across the room and switching on the TV, handing her the remote as he said, 'Keys? I shall need to get back in.'

She passed them over without a word, and when the front door clicked shut a few moments later exhaled a long breath of air. The day had taken on a life of its own; she had never felt so railroaded in all her born days. And she must look a mess.

The last thought prompted her to pull herself upwards, and she found by hitching and hotching along the walls and furniture the short journey to the bathroom wasn't too bad. She gazed at her reflection in the bathroom mirror. Her face was shiny and almost devoid of make-up, most of her mascara smudged under her eyes creating a faintly panda-style image. She groaned. Why on earth he wanted to stay and have dinner with her looking like this she didn't know!

She set to work feverishly, washing her face and then creaming it, before using just a touch of mascara on her lashes and careful foundation to take away her paleness. She brushed her hair until it curved in sleek wings against her cheeks, applied a few drops of her special French perfume, which cost an arm and a leg, and surveyed the results. Better, much better, but with her ankle throbbing like mad and her other leg protesting at the flamingo pose she'd had to adopt she really needed to sit down rather than get the plates ready.

Nevertheless, she struggled into her small but wonderfully compact little kitchen, flopping on one of the two pine stools and sitting limply for a moment or two. Her trousers were absolutely ruined; the nurse had slit the right leg to above her knee, and they were covered in dried mud from her fall. She didn't feel up to changing though, she decided as she fetched out plates, cutlery and wineglasses.

Ten minutes later she was ensconced at the small pine table in a corner of the sitting room, a gargantuan feast spread out before her and her wineglass full of orange juice—he was driving and she was on pain-killers that didn't mix with alcohol, Kingsley had informed her on his return with the food.

'Kingsley, this would feed a small army.' Rosalie gazed at the mixed hors d'oeuvres, beef with black peppers, pork in Kung po, chicken with ginger and pineapple, fried rice, prawn crackers and several other dishes crammed onto the table.

'I'm hungry.' He grinned at her, and her nerves jerked.

'Good, because I can't eat a quarter of this, let alone half,' she said evenly, refusing to relax her guard.

She wouldn't have believed how much food he could pack away if she hadn't seen it with her own eyes, and when the table was practically clear he fetched her painkillers without her asking him to, along with a glass of water. 'Thanks.' It was reluctant. She didn't need looking after, especially not by Kingsley Ward. She was well able to look after herself. And she refused to consider how nice it had felt.

He recognised the tone, but as she had the pallor of a ghost and was clearly bushed he let it go. 'Want me to help you get ready for bed?' he asked helpfully.

Grey eyes met blue, and when she saw the gleam in his she was forced to smile, albeit grudgingly. 'I can manage.'

'Do you want a coffee before I go?'

She shook her head.

'Tea? I know you English like your tea.'

'No, thanks.' Just *go*, for goodness' sake.

'Cocoa? Bovril? Ovaltine?' he offered.

'Nothing.' Not unless he wanted it thrown at him, that was.

'Correct me if I'm wrong, but I suspect I've outstayed my welcome,' he said with lazy self-mockery. And then he bent down, taking her hand and turning it over in his before he put his lips to her pink palm in a caress that was as fleeting as the previous kiss. 'Goodnight, Rosalie.' He straightened, still holding her hand. 'Sleep tight.'

'Goodnight.' Tingles were radiating from the point of contact with his mouth, but she was immensely proud of herself that she hadn't jerked away or shown any signs of the frantic thumping of her heart. 'Thank you for everything you've done today,' she added carefully, remembering her manners.

'It's a speciality of mine, damsels in distress.'

Her hand was her own again, and the return of it enabled her to smile fairly naturally before he turned and left the room. She heard the front door open, and then close with a click. She listened, her ears straining and her eyes narrowed.

He had gone.

CHAPTER FOUR

ROSALIE didn't know what she had expected after the fiasco of her day with Kingsley Ward, but it wasn't the ginormous basket of flowers that was delivered the next day with a card that simply said, 'Heal fast, K', followed by three weeks of no contact whatsoever.

For a week or so after the accident she had been as jumpy as a cricket, and, with the flowers scenting out her flat and acting as a constant reminder of Kingsley, she'd actually preferred being at the office. But at home or in the office, every telephone call had her heart beating fit to burst and her nerves jangling.

By the second week she had begun to wonder if she'd got all the signals wrong, and he wasn't interested in her at all except in her professional capacity.

By the third week she'd accepted her imagination had run away with itself, and he had just been acting out of kindness and concern. Kingsley was the type of man who would flirt mildly with any woman he was with, she told herself firmly on the Saturday morning as she dumped the wilting flowers in the bin. And the flowers had been a polite gesture of commiseration, nothing more. And as that was exactly what she wanted, it was all to the good, wasn't it? Of course it was.

Monday morning saw Mike calling for her in his top-of-the-range Jaguar as he'd done each morning since her accident. The crutches Jenny had obtained were fine for pottering about at work and home, but negotiating her way on crowded London pavements was a definite no-no. But it shouldn't be long till she had the plaster off now, Rosalie comforted herself as she plumped down in the passenger seat. Kingsley's doctor friend had sent her notes to her GP, and he in turn had arranged for any further treatment to be carried out at her local hospital. After a check-up the Friday before, they'd confirmed another two weeks and the plaster would be off. And it couldn't be a day too soon, Rosalie thought grumpily as the itching under the plaster, which had made itself felt for days now, made her wriggle in her seat.

'Something you might be interested in in this magazine.' As Mike slid into the car after helping her into her seat he reached over to the back seat and then threw a glossy magazine into Rosalie's lap. 'Hannah noticed it.'

'Oh, yes?' Hannah, Mike's wife, devoured periodicals ranging from gardening magazines right through to high fashion and everything in between. Mike had coined the word 'magaholic' with his wife in mind.

'Page with the corner turned down,' he said shortly before pulling out into the traffic.

Ridiculous, really, *really* ridiculous, but she felt as though someone had just punched her in the stomach as she gazed down at Kingsley in morning dress with a voluptuous brunette draped all over him. Painfully aware of Mike's studied nonchalance, she kept her face blank with tremendous effort, reading the short caption under each of the five photographs of the high society wedding in New York without commenting. It would appear he had been best man to a very old friend, a very rich old friend, and the brunette—who featured in each of the three photographs Kingsley was in—was the groom's baby sister and chief bridesmaid.

Rosalie got a measure of savage comfort from the fact that both the style and the colour of the bridesmaid's dress—citric yellow—did nothing for the girl in question. But then she was lovely enough for it not to matter too much, and the last picture—coyly captioned 'The best man taking his duties very seriously'—showed them wrapped in each other's arms so closely Rosalie was surprised the girl hadn't got in Kingsley's suit with him.

'Lovely dresses.' She slung the magazine over her shoulder back onto the seat. 'And Kingsley looked the part, didn't he?'

Mike darted her a quick glance before he said, 'There's talk that's the girl who's going to snare the ultimate bachelor.'

'Really.' It was cool. 'Lucky old bridesmaid.'

'Rosalie—' Mike stopped abruptly. 'Hell, I thought you should know,' he said irritably.

'Know?' She turned to him, stitching a smile on her face. 'Why on earth should I know, Mike? I shouldn't think the wedding, if there is one, would interfere with the job we're doing for him. Beyond that...' She shrugged.

'Yeah.' Mike was clearly out of his depth and she would have felt sorry for him in any other circumstances. As it was, she wanted to hit him. But why shoot the messenger? she asked herself in the next instant. And what was she getting all hot under the collar about anyway? Kingsley Ward was nothing to her, absolutely nothing.

She took a deep breath, turned to Mike and began to engage him in conversation about a couple of minor problems with Kingsley's job, as though this were just another ride to work.

The week went steadily down hill from that point, but finally it was Friday and the last few days of petty irritations, delays, broken promises—something builders excelled in—and general aggravation were over. She was spending the weekend with one of her aunts—her mother had had two sisters and, although Rosalie didn't see a great deal of them and their families, they were always there if she needed them—who lived in Kingston upon Thames, and as her aunt was collecting her at the office she had taken a weekend bag to work with her that morning.

She was deep into checking a list of figures and calculations at five o'clock when there was a knock at her door, and, Jenny having gone home early with a migraine, she called out, 'Come in, Beth. I won't be a sec.' Her aunt was only ten years older than Rosalie, and their relationship had always been one of friends on an equal level rather than a traditional aunt/niece affair. One of best friends even though their lives were different.

'I've been called a lot of things in my time, but never Beth.'

Her head shot up at the deep, amused voice from across the other side of the room. Her mouth dry, Rosalie said, 'Hello, Kingsley.' She was so glad she was sitting down.

'Hello, Rosalie,' he returned softly.

He was leaning against the open door, looking more attractive than any man had the right to. The Armani suit was not in evidence today, but the more casual light charcoal trousers and open-necked cornflower-blue shirt were killers. Or rather the body inside them was.

'I thought you were my aunt,' she said stupidly.

'But as you can see I am not.'

'No.' She sucked in a hidden breath, forcing a smile as she said, 'What can I do for you at this late hour?'

He strolled further into the room, his flagrant masculinity suddenly dwarfing the place, and to her horror he perched on the side of her desk as though he had the perfect right to sit wherever he liked. The ebony hair was even shorter than she remembered, the severity of the style emphasising his beautiful eyes with their almost feminine lashes. But of course he would have had it cut for the wedding, she thought testily. In order to look his best for...

'Do you mind?' She gestured at the papers covering the top of her desk. 'You might disturb them.'

He glanced at the papers and then raised his eyes to her face, keeping them there as her colour rose. 'What's the matter?' he asked quietly.

'Nothing is the matter,' she said coolly. 'I just don't want things muddled up, that's all.'

He folded his arms over his chest. 'I muddle you?'

'That's not what I meant.' And he knew it, darn him.

'How's the foot?' he asked softly.

'Much better.' She belatedly remembered her manners and added, 'Thank you for the flowers.'

'Your aunt? Are you seeing her tonight? I was hoping we could do dinner.' And he actually had the nerve to smile at her.

She didn't believe she was hearing this! He hadn't even bothered to contact her for weeks and then he breezed in expecting her to be available? To just drop everything?

'Sorry.' Her eyes narrowed coldly. 'I'm busy.'

'That's a shame.' Considering he had flown straight back across the Atlantic the moment the business deal he'd been setting up over the last weeks was in the bag. That, and Alexander's circus of a wedding. 'Are you free tomorrow?'

'I'm away for the weekend.' Funny, but it wasn't as satisfying to turn him down as she had imagined during the last few days when she had let her mind dwell on such a remote possibility occurring. In fact it wasn't satisfying at all.

'The aunt,' he said flatly. 'Right?'

She nodded. And then she did what she had promised herself she'd rather cut out her tongue than do, and said, 'How did the wedding go?' her voice as causal as she could make it.

'The wedding?' He showed his surprise but as far as she could determine there was no guilt in his eyes. The rat. 'Did I mention it before I went?'

He knew full well he hadn't; neither had he seen fit to call attention to Little Miss Canary. Rosalie shook her head. 'Mike's wife takes a magazine which covered the event,' she said pleasantly. 'You're famous, it seems.'

He grimaced. 'Alex is, you mean. He owns half of New York State, or rather the family do. He's a great guy but life in a goldfish bowl can get a little tedious.'

'I'm sure it can,' she said with no sympathy whatsoever.

'Okay, Rosalie.' He leant towards her, ignoring a couple of pages that drifted onto the floor. 'Why the big freeze?'

'I don't know what you mean,' she said stiffly.

'Sure you do.' His mouth had thinned but his voice was softer than ever. 'I ask you out to dinner and it's like I've committed the ultimate insult. No, thank you is simple enough surely?'

'You happen to be in London and at a loose end, and you expect me to fall on your neck with gratitude because you deign to offer to pass a couple of hours slumming?' she said tightly, regretting the words the second they had passed her lips. She had determined to be so cool and in control the next time she met him, and here she was practically demanding to know why she hadn't heard from him before this. Worst possible line to take, Rosalie, she

thought miserably, but she just couldn't seem to think
straight around this man.

'Is that what you think?' He had slid off the desk, moving round to her chair and pulling her to her feet regard-
less of her injured ankle. 'That you're a number in a little
black book?'

He had his hands on her forearms and she couldn't
move, but she raised her head defiantly, looking him full
in the face. 'Actually, yes.' And she made sure he knew
she meant it.

She waited for his temper to rise but he considered her
dryly, his head to one side. 'Some girls wouldn't mind
that,' he said softly. 'Being wined and dined with no
strings attached is what plenty of career women call for
these days. No messy complications or irritating ties.'

She didn't know quite how to answer that. 'You have
an answer for everything, don't you?' she muttered
crossly. Her voice wasn't as acidic as she would have
liked, mainly because, with the palms of her hands
pressed against his chest so hard she could feel the beat
of his heart, and the smell and feel of him all around her,
her head was beginning to spin.

'Do I?' There was a strange note in his voice, and when
he lifted a hand to her face, his fingertips caressing the
silk of her cheek, she was quite unable to move.

'Oh, I'm sorry!'

A flustered voice from the doorway brought Rosalie's
head jerking round, but Kingsley continued to hold her
for another moment or two before he turned, managing to
put an arm round her waist and pulling her firmly into
him as he did so.

'Beth.' Rosalie had never felt so rattled. 'I didn't hear
you come in. I mean—'

'You must be Rosalie's aunt.' Kingsley was all charm

as he deposited Rosalie gently back into her chair before
striding across the room with his hand outstretched towards the pretty, plump woman in the doorway. 'I'm
Kingsley Ward. How do you do? I was hoping to surprise
Rosalie and take her out to dinner, but it appears I'm too
late.'

He was all white teeth and winsome smiles, Rosalie
thought furiously, watching Beth go down before him like
a ninepin.

'Oh, what a shame.' Beth darted one quick glance towards Rosalie, who groaned inwardly at the delighted
gleam in her aunt's eye. Beth had been on at her for years
to find herself a nice man and enjoy life—the two were
synonymous in her aunt's mind—and Kingsley was
clearly the answer to all her hopes. 'Have you come far?'
she asked worriedly.

'New York.' He grinned winningly. 'Not too far.'

Beth wasn't going to be taken in by this drivel, was
she? It appeared she was.

'Really? But that's too bad. Look, Rosalie's coming to
us for the weekend; why don't you come too? We've a
couple of spare bedrooms now the children are all doing
their own thing. We've two at university and one's up in
Scotland doing goodness knows what on an archaeologi-
cal dig.'

'A dig, how interesting, but I couldn't impose…'

'It wouldn't be imposing, we'd absolutely love to have
you. Wouldn't we, Rosalie?' Beth was really going for it
now.

Two pairs of eyes looked her way; one pair earnest
brown, and the other alive with wicked blue delight. Rosalie warned herself her aunt had had a sheltered life and
might faint on the spot if she said what she was thinking.
'I'm sure Kingsley has things to do over the weekend,

Beth,' she said tightly. 'He's a very busy man.' She glared at him pointedly as she spoke.

'But all work and no play…' Beth beamed at the tall, dark and wonderfully handsome man in front of her. If she had gone out and sifted through all the men in London, she couldn't have found better for Rosalie, she thought happily. He was a hunk.

Oh, he plays all right. Boy, does he know how to play! Rosalie opened her mouth to set her aunt straight, but Kingsley was there before her. Wouldn't you just know it?

'If you are sure it's okay I would love to come,' he said with outrageous humility. 'I called here to see Rosalie straight from the airport so I've all my things in the car, as luck would have it. It'd be great to have a relaxing weekend.'

This was too much. Rosalie was almost choking with rage. And how could Beth invite him like this without checking with her first? But she knew how. Her aunt had been looking into those blue eyes and had lost all reason.

'Lovely.' Beth was almost wriggling like an ecstatic puppy. 'That's settled, then. And it will give you a chance to meet my husband, George—that's if we can manage to drag him out of his study. He's in the middle of preparing a paper on the origins of anthropomorphism, whatever that is.'

'The attribution of a human form or personality to a god or animal or thing, I think,' Kingsley supplied helpfully.

'Yes, that's right!' Beth gazed at him admiringly. 'Goodness, aren't you clever? You'll get on like a house on fire with George. He's a lecturer at City University and I think he despairs of intelligent conversation now the children have all flown the nest. They all take after him, you see, rather than me.'

'Then I'm sure that's their loss.'

She'd be sick if she listened to much more of this. Rosalie coughed meaningfully, and, having got their attention, said crisply, 'I'm sorry but I'll be another ten minutes finishing in here. Why don't you give Kingsley the address, Beth, and he can make his way later?' Which would enable her to fill her aunt in on the background to this crazy situation, and make it very clear any match-making possibilities were out of the window.

'Or why don't I disappear and do a bit of shopping I need to get, and see you both back at the house?' Beth put in cheerfully. 'You can show Kingsley—that's an unusual name, isn't it?'

She interrupted herself mid-flow, not an unknown occurrence for Beth. Kingsley smiled. 'My friends call me King, and I'm sure we're going to be friends?'

Beth giggled. 'King, it is, then. Gosh, how grand.'

Rosalie shut her eyes for an infinitesimal moment.

'Anyway, as I was saying, Lee can give you directions, then, if that's all right?' Beth continued. 'And I'll see you later.'

'That would be great. Thanks, Beth.' Kingsley turned to Rosalie, his eyes taking in her burning cheeks and hot eyes. 'I'll wait outside in your secretary's office until you've finished,' he said gently, ushering Beth out with him and shutting the door behind them both.

Rosalie stared at the door for a full ten seconds. Then she sagged back in her chair, the breath leaving her body in a long whoosh. She didn't know whether to laugh or cry, she thought helplessly. Who else but Kingsley would have managed that so perfectly for his own ends? He was amazing, and she didn't mean that in a laudatory sense either!

She lowered her gaze to the papers on her desk, but she had completely lost the thread of what she'd been doing, along with the will to continue. A weekend with Kingsley. This whole thing was surreal. And what about Tweety Pie? Where did she fit into the scheme of things? Was she one of those career women he had talked about who liked being wined and dined with no strings attached? Or were the rumours Mike had spoken about true and she was due to be the future Mrs Ward? Not that it made any difference to her, of course, Rosalie reassured herself in the next instant, but if the latter *was* the case he shouldn't be here right now.

She put her hands to her hot cheeks, her heart thumping a tattoo. She didn't want this, any of it. Panic rose, the taste acidic in her throat. She had made a life for herself, a good life, and she didn't want anyone or anything to spoil it. And Kingsley had the potential to do that.

She smoothed her hair away from her flushed face, aware her hands were shaking but unable to do anything about it.

Control. It was all about control, just as it had been with Miles. Miles had bulldozed his way into her life too, captivating and holding her with his charm and good looks and dominating her to the point where she had begun to believe black was white. She had been eighteen when she had met him and nearly twenty-one when they'd split up, and apart from the first few months of their relationship she'd existed rather than lived. Terrified of upsetting him, of losing his love; accepting always that she was the one to blame whatever the circumstances. *Her mother's daughter.*

She straightened, shame and humiliation making her

back rigid. Non-involvement spelt safety where a man like Kingsley was concerned, and she needed to remember that this weekend. This was just an amusing diversion for him, that was all.

It was another fifteen minutes before she left her office and by then Rosalie was in command of herself again. Kingsley glanced up from where he was sitting perched on the edge of Jenny's desk, leafing through a car magazine. He rose, slinging the magazine on a pile on the occasional table next to a comfy chair reserved for visitors, his voice expressionless as he said, 'Don't frown like that, you'll get lines before your time.'

Don't react, that's exactly what he wants. Rosalie's smile was brittle, her eyes cool, but she kept her voice pleasant. 'I'll take my chance.'

'You won't say that at fifty when you resemble a wrinkled prune instead of a peach.' He grinned at her, one of the grins she'd seen only once or twice, which touched the clear cold blue of his eyes with warm sunshine. It was hard to remain annoyed and try to freeze him in the face of such a metamorphosis, but she persevered.

And then strong arms caught her and he wasn't smiling any more. 'What was his name?' he asked softly.

'What?' She was so taken aback she made no move to free herself, her senses registering the shirt was made of silk as her hands rested against the wall of his chest.

'The guy who put the "Keep off" sign in place.'

Her eyes flickered. 'I haven't the faintest idea what you're talking about.' She looked at him defiantly.

'Liar.' His gaze moved over her face, burning where it touched. 'Someone's hurt you, and badly. What was his name?'

'Kingsley, let me go—'

'We can stand here all night like this if you like, but I

want to know his name.' And now the softness covered pure steel. 'The more I get to know you, the less I know you, and I don't like that.' The blue eyes were clear and steady and unrelenting.

She raised her head a fraction. 'I would have thought you are too busy to worry about me,' she said tightly.

He looked at her, his expression unreadable. 'Now something tells me you aren't referring to my work schedule,' he said quietly. 'Right?'

Darn right. She shrugged, attempting to move away, but the grip on her arms tightened. Now he was bullying her. Charming.

'And this is a follow-on from the little-black-book dig. Right again?' His voice was even and faintly quizzical.

'It was you who brought up the little black book,' she protested. 'I merely said—'

'I know what you said, Rosalie.'

He lowered his head and kissed her. His mouth was urgent, hungry, and this kiss was as different from anything that had gone before as ice from fire. She made a brief movement of withdrawal but then as it continued, his mouth slowly and deeply taking what it wanted, she felt desire rise hotly in the core of her being. She felt weightless, the feel of him and the warmth of his body causing her to melt into him even as a tiny part of her mind that was still capable of rational thought warned her that this was madness.

His hands were stroking the silky skin of her back under the thin blouse she was wearing, his fingers delicately exploring even as they urged her closer into him. She could feel what the kiss was doing to him, and it was sweet, potent, to know she could arouse him so easily.

It was the ringing of the telephone on Jenny's desk that penetrated the world of touch and taste that had taken her over, and Rosalie had no idea how long they had been standing wrapped in each other's arms. As the answer machine took a message from someone concerning an account problem, Kingsley said softly, 'I wouldn't kiss you like that if I was involved with someone else, Rosalie. Oh, I might take you out to dinner or for a drink, a date where everything remained on the level, but there would be no lovemaking.'

'Just platonic friendship?' She tried to make her voice lightly disbelieving, but she was trembling too much.

'Just so.'

Did she believe him? She stared into the piercingly blue eyes and admitted she didn't know. She had believed Miles and look where that had got her. The thought of Miles caused her heart to give an unsteady slam, and something of the impact must have registered in her eyes because Kingsley said, 'Sooner or later you have to put a toe in the water again; you know that, don't you?'

It didn't dawn on her what she had admitted when she said, 'Why do I?' until much later.

'Because you are far too beautiful and desirable not to, that's why. Whoever he was, Rosalie, and whatever he did, the future is yours and what you make of it. Do you believe that?'

She remained silent, the euphoria of how it had felt to be in his arms, to be kissed by him, gone. And then she said very quietly, 'His name was Miles Stuart.'

There was a second of stillness. It seemed to go on for ever.

'And?' he said gently. Very gently.

'And we met when I was eighteen, married when I was nineteen and were getting divorced when I was twenty-one.' Her voice was louder now, her face painfully defiant. Story done.

'When you were at university?' he persisted softly.

She nodded. This was as far as she was going to go.

Kingsley Ward had had fifteen ruthlessly hard years of experience in the market place of big business to know all about keeping poker-faced, and this came to his aid now, enabling him to maintain an impassive countenance as he said, 'And he hurt you?' knowing he really had no right to ask.

'I don't want to talk about it.' It was unmistakably final.

He took a deep breath, finding his guts had twisted like a corkscrew. 'Fine,' he said calmly, 'but what I said earlier still stands. He is the past, you have to look to the present.'

He didn't have a clue what he was talking about. Rosalie looked at him steadily. Decisions and consequences was a rotten game to lose at eighteen years old.

'Have you had therapy?' he asked after a moment or two.

'This is England, not America.' It was too sharp and she moderated her voice when she said, 'Like I said, I don't want to talk about it.'

'But you have talked it through with someone? At the time, when it all happened, or later?' he said quietly.

Rosalie could hear the beat of her own heart. She didn't want to think about Miles, not even for a second. It made her feel sick. She swallowed audibly. 'I'm not like that,' she said carefully. 'It wouldn't have helped.' In fact it would have killed her; it still would, even ten years later. There were some things so degrading that to share them with another human being was unthinkable. 'I married him and it was a mistake, that is all anyone needs to know.'

The hell it was. Kingsley nodded. 'Sure,' he said easily, 'whatever. But coming back to us—'

'Us?' Where did us come from?

There was real panic in her voice and now his tone was velvety smooth when he said, 'There's an us, Rosie, whether you like it or not. There was from the moment we laid eyes on each other. Call it the X-factor or whatever you like, but your body knew what it wanted long before you could bring your mind to accept it.' His eyebrows rose, daring her to disagree.

'You're talking sex,' she said flatly. 'That's all.'

Blue eyes glinted. 'Sex is spelt with three letters; it's not a four-letter word, Rosie.'

'Don't call me Rosie. Everyone shortens Rosalie to Lee.' A small point but somehow vitally important.

And then Kingsley hit the nail on the head and summed up what she was feeling when he said softly, 'But I'm not everyone, am I?'

Her skin shivered. No, he wasn't.

'Besides which, Lee is cold, abstract, almost boyish. Rosie is warm and soft and as sexy as hell.' He bent and picked up her crutches from where they'd fallen seconds after he had taken her mouth. 'But enough of this getting to know each other,' he said dryly. 'Beth will be waiting at home for us.'

'I can't believe you virtually invited yourself along this weekend,' she muttered, disturbingly aware that she seemed to have lost on every twist and turn of this conversation.

'Believe it.' He eyed her unrepentantly. 'And you ain't seen nothing yet, Rosie. Trust me on that if nothing else.'

CHAPTER FIVE

THE June evening was warm with all the delicious smells of summer when Kingsley's car drew into Beth and George's pebbled drive, and Rosalie got an inordinate amount of pleasure from the fact that Kingsley was speechless for once. She hadn't warned him what to expect, and it was clear the quaint old thatched cottage engulfed in roses, honeysuckle and jasmine, and set in a perfectly Victorian garden, had stunned him.

'What a place.' He turned to her after a moment or two, his voice richly appreciative.

'Gorgeous, isn't it?' They hadn't said much on the way and it was a relief for some of the crackling tension to diffuse. 'The back garden is just as beautiful. It's full of hollyhocks and wallflowers and all the old-fashioned types of flowers. I've always thought of this place as a piece of heaven on earth. A very English heaven, of course,' she added with a smile.

'Wooden benches and a rose garden and arbours?' he said smilingly. 'I bet it has all those?'

She nodded. 'And rambling roses scaling old stone walls and apple and plum trees. It's just perfect—to me, that is.'

'It must be worth a small fortune,' he said softly, glancing at the mullioned windows. 'I didn't realise lecturers were paid so well over here.'

'They're not. George's father was something big in the city, a real wheeler and dealer, which is pretty amazing to think about when you meet George. He's a dear but hardly of this world, such a genius in his own field he doesn't know what day it is most of the time. Beth's perfect for him; she's more mother than wife. Anyway, as the only child he got everything when his parents died in a car accident just after he and Beth married, and so they decided to plough the lot into their own little piece of English heaven which is near enough the university for it not to be a huge problem. Of course that was over two decades ago now, and the price of property has gone crazy since then. As an investment it was pretty cute. I think George's father would have been proud of him for once!'

'Undoubtedly.' He turned fully to face her in the tight confines of the car as he reached out a hand and touched the shining silk of her hair, letting one finger trail down the smooth skin of her cheek. 'Real peaches and cream,' he murmured almost to himself, 'and very English. And yet the French side is apparent too.' Rosalie had told him during the wait at the hospital some weeks before that both her parents had died when she was young, but that was all, and now he asked, 'Your parents? Was it an accident like George's parents or something similar?'

She answered the way the family had decided to handle it at the time of her father's suicide. 'My mother died of a brain haemorrhage, and my father felt he couldn't go on without her...'

'He took his own life?' he said very quietly.

She nodded, flushing slightly. She had never found it hard before to leave out the more pertinent facts that clothed the bare truth in quite a different garment, but now she felt uncomfortable. Therefore it was with a real sense of relief that she saw Beth at the front door beckoning them into the house. 'Beth's calling us.'

She turned to open her door but he caught her hand for

a second, saying quietly, 'You've had a tough start in life one way or the other.'

'People have worse.' He was making her feel twice as guilty. 'My grandparents were wonderful to me, and my mother's two sisters spoilt me rotten. You might meet Jeanne—she normally calls round if she knows I'm here, like Beth does if I visit Jeanne. She lives quite close.'

Why had she said that? It was too cosy. As if he were her boyfriend or something. She didn't want him to meet her relatives, or know all about her. She pulled away from him now, cross with herself and everyone else. She had always been so careful to keep the opposite sex at a distance since Miles, even the harmless ones, and now she was in the most farcical situation and through no fault of her own. Beth might be one of the warmest and most hospitable creatures under the sun, but right at this moment she wasn't in the mood to appreciate her aunt's generosity.

She hoped George and Kingsley would take an instant dislike to each other, and Kingsley would be bored stiff here. She always spent time with Beth when she visited, knowing how lonely her aunt got with the children gone and George ensconced in his study most of the time he wasn't at the university, and she saw no reason to change things because Kingsley had engineered an invite. Perhaps he'd give up and leave early if things were too dull? He was used to the jet-set lifestyle, after all.

'You're frowning again.' Kingsley had come round to the passenger door, opening it and helping her out, and now his voice was soft when he added, 'Smile sweetly for Beth. We don't want to upset your lovely aunt, do we?'

She murmured a word that was rude enough to make him blink, and, encouraged at that small victory, stitched a smile on her face as she hobbled off towards the front door, cursing the plaster and the fact she couldn't sweep elegantly in front of him.

George and Kingsley did not take an instant dislike to each other at all. Kingsley displayed such an interest in the other man's work that George was in danger of becoming positively effusive over pre-dinner cocktails, and Rosalie groaned inwardly as she contemplated her aunt's gratified expression, for all the world like a satisfied mother whose brilliant child was being appreciated.

'I'm just going to show Kingsley the garden.' When she couldn't stand it a minute more, Rosalie put down her cocktail and all but frogmarched him out through the open French doors and into the last of the spangled evening sunshine.

'You don't have to humour him quite so enthusiastically, you know,' she said snappily once they were far enough away from the house not to be overheard.

'I'm interested,' he protested mildly, pulling her down onto a sun-warmed bench near an old tree providing a giant sculpture for sweet-smelling roses to ramble over. 'Sit awhile and relax, you're too tense,' he added reprovingly. 'You need to learn to chill out.'

Chill out? *Chill out?* She might have got some very nice chilling-out time this weekend, but with Kingsley around relaxing was not an option. She'd never felt so edgy in all her life.

A couple of blue tits were busy stocking up for the night from a nut feeder Beth had hanging from the tree, and Rosalie kept her gaze on the small birds, willing herself to calm down. She had a whole weekend to get through; she couldn't afford to let him get to her like this.

Nevertheless, she was painfully aware of him sitting

next to her, one arm stretching along the back of the old wooden bench so that his body was inclined towards her. She had noticed the faint dark shadow of body hair under the blue shirt earlier, and now the delicious scent of him she had smelt once or twice before teased her nostrils, forcing her to acknowledge her heightened senses.

Kingsley stretched out his long legs, his voice easy as he said, 'This is great, isn't it? You could believe the rest of the world didn't exist here, it's so peaceful.'

'I wouldn't have thought you were the sort of man who wanted peace.' It slipped out and she regretted it immediately.

'No?' He bent closer, turning her face to him. 'Why is that?'

Rosalie flushed. 'Just your reputation,' she said after a moment. But she knew he would persist with this now.

'Which is?' He didn't seem inclined to let go of her chin.

'Work hard and play hard.'

'Ah, I see.' She wasn't quite sure what he saw, but then he said, 'Amazingly I'm not a robot, Rosie. I get tired, I get sick on occasion, scratch me and I bleed, just like any other man.'

She lowered her eyes; the intensity of his gaze was unnerving 'I know that,' she said awkwardly. 'Of course I know that.'

'I don't think you do.' He let go of her, and they continued to sit without speaking in the warm, scented air. Fat honey-bees buzzed busily among the profusion of flowers, paying special attention to the roses, and the evening was alive with bird song. Why had she never brought Miles here? Her hands were clasped too tightly together and she forced herself to relax her fingers one by one. Had it been because university life had been so frantic, so busy, their circle of friends so absorbing? Or because she had been frightened the cracks in their relationship, which had begun to appear shortly after the quick register office wedding, would have been apparent to Beth? That her aunt would have recognised the same spirit of tyranny and oppression in Miles that had been in her sister's husband?

She shifted slightly on the seat, brushing a wisp of hair from her face. But at least her father had had some excuse for acting as he had, or not an excuse, exactly, she corrected herself, but a reason behind his actions that explained his obsessive peremptoriness with her mother. And he had loved her too, tortured and twisted as that love had become. Miles had been the original spoilt little rich kid, the adored and indulged only son whose every whim had been granted since birth.

'You haven't left him behind yet, have you?' The voice at her side was very quiet, and as Rosalie's eyes shot up to meet his Kingsley covered her hand with one of his own, refusing to let go of it when she tried to pull away. 'He's right here now, isn't he?' he said softly. 'The silent spectre at our shoulders.'

Rosalie's stomach clenched. She looked away, her mouth unconsciously tightening. How come he could read her mind?

'Do you still love him?' Kingsley said evenly.

'Love him?'' It carried such distaste Kingsley couldn't doubt her antipathy.

So, he'd been barking up the wrong tree there. He knew a second of quick relief, before the question of what *was* wrong kicked in. 'So you don't still care for him. Why is he such a big deal in your life, then?'

'I told you before, I don't want to talk about Miles,'

she said shakily, her voice refusing to obey the command to be firm and cool. 'I'm cold, let's go in.'

'No, you're not,' he challenged softly, squeezing her hand as he spoke. 'And I'm just trying to understand where you're coming from, that's all. I don't want to drag up painful memories for the sake of it, but right from the first moment I met you there's always been a silent third party present. I didn't know what the problem was at first, but it's him, the ex, isn't it?'

He felt the withdrawal even though she hadn't moved a muscle and he knew he was right. He also knew he was getting in way over his head. This wasn't the way he did things. He cursed himself for being a fool. He had done the love and commitment thing once and had been left with enough egg on his face to keep him in omelettes for the rest of his life.

'You've no right to question me like this.'

She was damn right, he hadn't. 'Yes, I have,' he said grimly. 'You're here right now with me, not him, and I don't like threesomes.'

The control thing again. He couldn't have said anything worse as far as she was concerned. They were all the same under the skin, the whole male race, apart from the occasional being from another planet like George. 'I didn't invite you to be here, remember?' she bit back harshly.

'Do you want me to leave?' he asked grimly.

Did she? It was a drenching shock to find out it was the last thing in all the world she wanted, and it caused her to say, her voice quivering despite all her efforts to control it, 'Yes, that's exactly what I want.'

The world was motionless, and then with a low growl of irritation he took her into his arms. He kissed her over and over until her weak, fluttering protests faded, each kiss deeper and hungrier than the one before, and somehow she found herself lying on his lap with her hands clinging to his shoulders. And still he kissed her. His mouth was warm and wonderfully experienced and his arms were strong, the heat between them explosive.

It was Beth's voice calling from the house that eventually brought them apart, Rosalie blinking and staring at him with huge drugged eyes as he raised his head. 'You don't want me to leave,' he whispered gently, his eyes so blue it hurt her to look into them. 'Say it.' He kissed the tip of her nose, a tender, curiously intimate caress. 'Say it, Rosie.'

She looked at him. 'I don't want you to leave.'

'Good.' As Beth's voice called again he stood up with her, lowering her gently to her feet before reaching down and handing her the crutches. 'That's good, because I had no intention of going away.' He grinned at her, purposely breaking the spell that their lovemaking had woven round them because they had to go into the house and pretend the world hadn't suddenly tilted and changed direction. 'And for the rest of the weekend we're just going to enjoy being in each other's company and have fun,' he added softly. 'Okay? No more questions, no more big debates.'

She blinked again. He was like a human chameleon, changing his persona so swiftly and completely she couldn't keep up with him, she thought helplessly.

And as though he had read her mind, his smile faded. 'There's nothing to be afraid of,' he said quietly. 'We're two adult people getting to know each other a little better and neither of us is hurting anyone else. What is wrong with that?'

Put like that, nothing. But one of the adults was Kingsley Ward, which took this into a vastly different ball game.

'Come on.' As though he had suddenly tired of the

situation Kingsley's voice was brisk. 'I'm starving. I hope Beth's a good cook.'

'She's a brilliant cook.' This was safer ground. 'Three super-intelligent children and a near genius husband inspired her to excel in the thing she's always had a gift for, and her meals are second to none. Even your friend, Glen, would have a hard job to compete. And she's something of a wine boff too.'

Kingsley smiled again, a very cat-with-the-cream smile. 'I think I'm going to enjoy this weekend in more ways than one,' he said softly. 'Wine, woman and song.'

'Shouldn't that be wine, *women* and song?' Rosalie said breathlessly, taking a second to stop and brush back the hair from her face as they walked to the house, her crutches proving a mixed blessing, as always.

He let his eyes roam over the high, rounded breasts, slender waist and long, long legs, before lifting his gaze to the beautiful face with its curtain of shining chestnut hair. 'Not from where I'm standing,' he said gruffly.

The meal was as delicious as Rosalie had promised, and, with the wine flowing as freely as the conversation, and even George cracking a couple of jokes and proving quite witty in Kingsley's company, Rosalie found she was enjoying herself.

Kingsley had a way with people, she thought towards the dessert stage of the dinner, watching Beth positively bask in his appreciative comments about the food, which had actually prompted George to take a break from Planet Antiquity long enough to give his wife a rare compliment. But then Miles had always been able to charm the birds out of the trees too.

The thought was like a punch in the chest and she was angry with herself for letting Miles intrude into her thoughts once again. She hadn't thought about him in a long time, and now it seemed he was at the back of her mind all the time, or, as Kingsley had said, a spectre at her shoulder. *Was* Kingsley like her ex?

She surveyed him from across the table as he held Beth and George captivated with another of the many funny stories he'd related during the evening, the sting in the tail often being directed against himself.

Certainly Miles hadn't been able to laugh at himself, but then Kingsley was probably quite aware that it was a definite plus in winning people over, she thought, with no apology for the cynicism.

Miles had been tall, dark and handsome—like Kingsley. Rich—like Kingsley. Possessed of the certain something that, along with wealth and power, proved to be an almost irresistible draw to the average female—like Kingsley.

Miles had also been cruel and unreasonable, a harsh despot who hid his true nature under blindingly good looks and a winsome boyish manner. He had been the perfect man until they had got married, the catch of the university, and she'd known all her friends had been green with envy. Who would have believed that behind locked doors he could turn into a vicious, brutal sadist when crossed, a savage, and for something as trivial as his toast being burnt? The flat they had rented had become a place of terror, and it had got so she had only felt safe when she'd been at her lectures or out in a group with their friends.

Why had she stuck it as long as she had? Probably because she'd believed marriage was for life back then, and she had been desperate to make it work after what had happened to her parents. Every time he had hurt her she'd told herself she had to try that bit harder to be a better wife. It had to be her that was at fault, surely? Miles was perfect; everyone said so. And then had come the night of their graduation…

'…don't you think, Lee?'

She came out of the horror to see Beth's dining table and three pairs of eyes looking at her. 'I'm sorry.' She forced a smile. 'Thinking about a problem at work.'

'Not my job, I hope?' Kingsley's voice was easy, lazy, but the piercing blue of his eyes told her she hadn't done quite such a good cover-up job as she'd have liked.

'Yours is fine.' She turned her gaze to Beth, who had been the one who had spoken her name. 'Sorry,' she said again. 'What were you saying?'

The conversation progressed naturally from that point, but Rosalie was aware that, although he laughed and joked as before, Kingsley's gaze was thoughtful when it rested on her.

They didn't reach the coffee and liqueur stage until just before midnight, and by then the conflicting emotions Rosalie had suffered since Kingsley had walked into her office had her aching for sleep. Fortunately Beth and George were normally in bed by ten, and once everyone had finished their coffee and brandy Beth made no bones about retiring.

The four of them walked up the exquisite curved staircase the cottage sported together, and once on the landing Beth and George disappeared into the master suite after the customary goodnights, leaving Kingsley and Rosalie alone on the landing.

'Goodnight, Rosie.' He had bent his dark head and captured her mouth before she could react. Warmth spread through her, and then a rising passion, the blood rushing through her body like hot mulled wine. He had pulled her hard into him, kissing her with almost violent intensity before he suddenly let her go.

Her legs were trembling as he held her away from him so she could stabilise herself, and he looked at her with hungry eyes. 'There was a woman once, when I was twenty, and I got my fingers burnt badly,' he said roughly. 'Since then I've always been up-front about how I feel; no promises of for ever, no commitment beyond that whilst the affair lasts I'll be faithful and I expect the lady to be. Honesty and loyalty, and no regrets, no recriminations. Not a bad philosophy, is it?'

She stared at him. What was he saying, that he wanted an affair with her? A no-strings-attached kind of affair? For a moment her brain wouldn't work, and then she side-stepped the issue by saying, 'And the women are happy with that?'

'Of course.' He sounded surprised she had asked. 'When you get down to basics most women acknowledge that love might sound a pleasant concept but it just doesn't work in the real world. Sooner or later mistrust and doubt rear their ugly heads, and if you find out your partner has been cheating on you...' He shrugged. 'It happens. All the time. The divorce rate is evidence of that. Sexual compatibility is something else. That's real and honest and not reliant on trusting someone or being trusted.'

Rosalie took a deep breath. 'Are you propositioning me, Kingsley?' she asked expressionlessly.

'You want me, Rosie. And I want you—from the first second I laid eyes on you I've been burning up with the need. You're single, I'm single. It's the most natural thing on earth.'

She wasn't sure how she felt exactly, but she knew she wanted to hit him, and that didn't seem quite fair when he was being so honest. She tried for lightness. 'Sorry, but I don't do affairs,' she said pleasantly.

'I know that.' He pulled her closer again, his palms cupping her sides and his fingertips splaying over her lower ribs. 'And I respect how you feel.'

She could feel his strength and warm virility flowing into her, and the lure of it made her voice husky when she said, 'But? And don't tell me there isn't a but. ''But'' this is different. ''But'' we'd be so good for each other. ''But'' it's not often people have the empathy we have. Am I right?'

For an answer he moved, pressing her back against the wall of the landing, holding her there with his body as he took her mouth again. His thighs were hard against hers and she could feel every inch of him as he drained her will to protest, his mouth and tongue fuelling the burning desire that had exploded the moment his lips had touched hers. She could feel his heart pounding like a sledgehammer, mirroring her pulse, and for a second the urge to give in, to open the door of her bedroom and pull him in with her was paramount.

It was enough to shock her back to reality. Her arms had been round his waist but now she brought them up to his chest and pushed, her voice shaking as she said, 'Don't. I don't want this, Kingsley. Let me go.'

Kingsley had known many women over the years and thought he understood the female species pretty well, but the fear in Rosalie's voice stunned him. He stopped instantly, taking a backwards step that removed his body from hers, but kept his arms outstretched either side of her body, holding her within the circle of his maleness. 'What the hell did he do to you?' he asked softly, his voice very deep. And then, at the look on her white face, he straightened. 'Okay, okay, I know. You don't want to talk about it.'

'I can't.' It was a whisper. 'I can't talk about it.'

'You don't trust me enough.' His expression was unreadable.

'I don't know you,' she said truthfully. And yet part of her felt as though she had known him all her life, which was even more scary. Petrifying, in fact.

His brow furrowed, and she could almost see the formidably astute and intelligent brain considering the implications of what she had said. Then he nodded, his face giving nothing away as to what he was thinking. 'I can accept that,' he said after a moment or two. 'So we remedy the situation.'

She stared at him. 'What do you mean?' she asked warily.

He smiled, his astonishing eyes as warm as cornflowers in a sun-drenched meadow. 'We date for a while,' he said matter-of-factly. 'Nothing heavy, we can take it as slow as you want, but I'll be there for you and you'll be there for me.' His American accent was very strong suddenly.

'I don't think—'

'This is not a suggestion, Rosie.' Now the blue gaze resembled cool water. 'It's either that or I kiss you until we end up in bed together right now. And I could do it with very little resistance from you if I put my mind to it.'

Arrogant swine. She was furious at the picture he'd painted but at the same time her innate honesty forced her to accept he had a point. Certainly she wasn't confident enough in her powers to resist him to put it to the test, anyway. She contented herself with a glare, before she said, 'This dating? A kiss goodnight at the end of the evening is all you'll get, so if you're thinking—'

'I said we would take it as slow as you want.' He was standing with his legs slightly apart and his powerful arms folded over his chest, and he looked big. Big and rugged and so incredibly sexy it made her mouth dry. 'Contrary to what you so obviously believe, I can actually wine and dine a woman without expecting a pay-off at the end of the date,' he added dryly.

No doubt because his dates in the past had been panting to get him in the hay! She cleared her throat. It was only fair to put him in the picture. 'Look, since…since Miles I haven't dated,' she said flatly, dropping her eyes from his and staring at the carpet because it made it easier to say what she needed to say. 'And I don't want to get into another relationship again, not ever. I have my work and my home and—'

'And you are perfectly happy to coast the rest of your life; no highs, no lows, just flat, calm water endlessly in view?' he drawled softly. 'I don't think so, Rosie.'

'How would you know?' she shot back indignantly, her eyes shooting up to meet the slightly taunting gaze. 'You don't know me.'

'We seem to have completed a full circle.' He studied her face, the confusion she was trying to hide apparent in the dusky darkness of her eyes. 'And I suspect every avenue of argument would come back to the same thing. So…we date. No discussion, no debate about it, we do it. All right?'

And with that he turned, reaching out for the handle of his door and opening it without another word before he stepped into the room and closed the door quietly behind him.

She didn't believe this! Rosalie stood for a few moments more, glancing almost pleadingly about the cool, gracious landing as though it were going to provide an answer to her bemusement. Kingsley Ward was as male as you could get—aggressive, strong, ruthless and possessed of a sexual magnetism that was as powerful as it was formidable. He was the last man on earth she should date. So how come she found herself in a position where she was doing just that?

She shook her head at herself, going back in her mind over their conversation to see where she had slipped up.

'Oh, to heck with it.' She glared one last time at his closed door, hoping it would penetrate the wood and pin him where he stood, and shrugged her shoulders. She could refuse the dates when they occurred—or at least a number of them—once this crazy weekend was over. Give him the cold shoulder. Freeze him out.

It was scant comfort. Possibly because she didn't believe it. To date, trying to freeze Kingsley out had been about as successful as a snowball surviving in hell.

Whatever, she'd cope. She squared her shoulders, entering her own room and determining to ignore the fact that Kingsley was right next door, possibly getting undressed, or perhaps even naked in the shower? Enough. She banished the erotic images before they had a chance to take hold.

Yes, she would cope. She had survived Miles Stuart, hadn't she? Not only survived him, but gone on to make something of herself and carve out her own life on her own terms. So she could hold her own with Kingsley. She wasn't a trusting, nervous little eighteen-year-old now, bowled over by the fact that the most gorgeous boy she had ever seen said he wanted to love her and take care of her.

Take care of her... She flopped down onto the bed, dropping the crutches on the floor. Miles had taken care of her all right, taken care that she came close to a nervous breakdown, damn it.

But Kingsley was right about one thing—Miles *was* the past. She nodded to herself, the churning in her stomach the stark memories always caused making itself known. But if Kingsley thought he had taken out a contract for an affair when he'd signed her up to work for him, he was wrong. Her eyes narrowed and she looked resolutely ahead, her gaze inward-looking. Boy, was he ever wrong…

CHAPTER SIX

THE next day Rosalie was awoken at seven in the morning by a distraught Beth. The dean at their youngest son's university had rung. He had been careful what he'd said, but it had transpired one of the students in Jeff's block had been diagnosed with meningitis and was now in isolation at the local hospital. All the other students had been put on antibiotics as a precautionary measure, but three of them—of whom Jeff was one—were unwell. There was no need to panic, the dean had assured Beth, but to be on the safe side they had also been taken to the hospital and some tests were being run.

'We're going straight to Cambridge now.' Beth was all but pulling her hair out. 'Will you and Kingsley be all right? There's plenty of food in the fridge and freezer, but could you possibly feed the cats at six tonight? Tuna in sunflower oil, it's in the right-hand kitchen cupboard over the sink. And they like full cream milk and will only eat and drink off their china saucers. They'll be turning up wanting milk soon, no doubt.'

'They'll be fine, we'll look after them.' Rosalie thought it was just like Beth to worry about the cats rather than her guests at a time like this. Beth was primarily concerned with the needy and vulnerable, which was one of the reasons Rosalie loved her so much, but she had always thought that her aunt's anxiety over the cats—two enormously fat, amber-eyed females with filthy tempers—was misplaced. If ever anything could look after itself, those two could.

'We'll probably stay in a hotel somewhere overnight and see how things are tomorrow, but I'll ring you.' Beth gazed at her with tragic eyes. 'Oh, Lee, I'm so worried.'

'Jeff will be fine, I'm sure of it. Now you go and Kingsley and I will look after things here.'

Rosalie tried to be encouraging as she saw Beth off, and she had just made her way into the kitchen to make a cup of tea when she became aware of a presence behind her. She turned sharply, almost losing her balance as her plaster foot slid on the terracotta tiles, and Kingsley smiled at her from his vantage point in the doorway. 'Hi.'

'Hello.' She instantly became aware of the fact that she hadn't even brushed her hair in the mad scramble to get her aunt out of the house before Beth completely went to pieces, and the nightie and thin robe she was wearing were not her prettiest ones.

Kingsley, on the other hand, had obviously recently showered as his damp hair bore witness to, but he hadn't shaved. His stubble was dynamite. As were the midnight-blue silk robe and matching pyjama bottoms, which emphasised every line and contour of the hard, powerful body in a way that should be illegal. The robe was pulled loosely together, the casually tied belt allowing a tantalising glimpse of his thickly muscled torso and the silky black hair on his chest, and his whole demeanour was one of contented ease. He was a man very much at ease with his own body, that much was for sure, but the overwhelming maleness was such that Rosalie found her throat was dry and her hands were damp.

'Tea?' It was a squeak and she heard it with annoyance.

'Coffee, if that's okay.'

Of course, she should have known.

'The instant variety will do,' he offered helpfully as she made a move towards Beth's coffee percolator. 'As long as it's hot and strong first thing in the morning I'm not fussy.' He strolled fully into the kitchen as he spoke, and her senses went into hyperdrive. Beth's kitchen wasn't small, in fact it was the sort of oak-beamed old country kitchen that would accommodate a whole London flat in its cavernous depths, but suddenly it had shrunk alarmingly.

She hastily explained about Beth and George's sudden departure, opening one of the big windows as she talked and letting in the cats, who had been prowling up and down the windowsill for a few moments. They trod delicately over the draining-board and jumped neatly onto the floor—obviously an old and practised route into the house—and then both of them began to wind themselves round Kingsley's legs, purring loudly.

The air was clean and fresh as it poured into the room, the sun already warm, and the cheerful twittering of the birds in the surrounding trees and bushes almost drowned out the sound of the boiling kettle.

'They like you.' She gestured to the cats, who had continued their elegant homage even though Kingsley was now perched on the edge of the massive old kitchen table, his long legs ensuring his feet still touched the floor. 'They aren't normally so friendly'.

'Perhaps you should take a leaf out of their book,' he suggested in a lightly mocking tone. And then as her foot slipped again he said firmly, 'Sit down, I'll do it.'

She sat down, mainly because the pure male sensuality was a little unnerving at just after seven in the morning when she hadn't quite got her armour in place.

'Toast? Cereal?' He placed a cup of tea in front of her as he spoke, his tall, lean frame lending itself surprisingly easily to the domestic scene. 'Or eggs done the Ward way?'

She eyed him suspiciously. 'Which is?'

'Nothing more alarming than scrambled with butter and onion, and served on toasted bread with a slice of bacon or ham. Delicious, even if I do say so myself.'

'You cook?' She almost added 'too?' and stopped herself just in time. His ego was already jumbo size; she didn't need to add to it. No doubt plenty of women did that already.

'Of course.' He grinned at her. 'As long as you want eggs the Ward way, that is.'

'For breakfast, dinner and tea?' she guessed dryly.

'You've got it.' Blue eyes laughed and she had to join in.

Oh, help, why did he have to be so drop-dead gorgeous? It was first thing in the morning and he looked good enough to eat, whereas she probably resembled something that had been pulled through a hedge backwards. Perhaps he'd go off the idea of them dating now he'd seen her in all her morning glory? Funny, but the thought wasn't comforting.

However, Kingsley didn't seem put off by the gargoyle at the table as he lifted a strand of hair from her face, letting it run through his fingers as he said almost absently, 'Raw silk, and such beautiful colours when the sun catches it. Who do you get your colouring from?'

'My father. He had grey eyes too.'

There was a tightness to her voice that hadn't been there moments before but he didn't comment on it, merely letting his fingertips rest against the smooth skin before he turned abruptly. 'Four eggs for me. How many for you?'

'Two would be heaps.'

She watched him as he found and prepared the onions first, cutting them expertly under a little water before drying them and adding them to the fat sizzling in the frying-pan. 'Now whilst they're browning it's time for the toast.'

He turned as he spoke, smiling at her, and she was aware her breathing became quick and shallow. This was too nice, too delicious. Forget the food, she could feast for ever just looking at his body as he moved with an animal grace that was pure magic.

'As you're in charge of the food, the cats want breakfast,' she said dryly, hiding her trembling under a veneer of nonchalance.

'Of course. Are they boys or girls?' he said lazily.

'With names like Meg and Polly, girls, I hope. Either that or they're very confused felines.'

'Then I know just the thing.' He dived into the back of Beth's enormous fridge and came out with a carton of cream. He poured a little into an earthenware dish before she could tell him about the china saucers, but wouldn't you just know it, she thought helplessly, the darn cats lapped it up nevertheless.

'Don't know a woman in the world who can resist cream,' he said, turning to the onions and moving them around the pan with a wooden spoon.

'And of course you know most of them,' she said sweetly.

'Miaow.' He glanced at her for just a second, the blue eyes glittering. 'Meg and Polly are ashamed of you, you're giving cats a bad name.'

She stuck out her tongue at him and he grinned again, adding the beaten eggs to the onion and putting the lid on the frying pan whilst he buttered the toast, and cut several slices of ham from a joint he had found in the fridge. 'This is delicious.' Some of the ham had found its way into his mouth. 'Beth's rolled it in brown sugar, by the look of it, and perhaps a touch of mustard. I could get used to living here, given half a chance.'

She took a big gulp of her tea. As a hard businessman and entrepreneur he had been pretty devastating, and the side of him she'd seen the evening before had knocked her for six, but this morning the domestic Kingsley, clothed in the silk robe and pyjama bottoms, was every maiden's prayer. How could anyone make cooking so sexy? she asked herself breathlessly. He could knock all those TV chefs off the face of the planet.

By the time he placed a heaped plate in front of her, along with a glass of ice-cold orange juice, she had expended enough nervous energy to be absolutely starving. 'This is wonderful.' There was a note of surprise in her voice.

'Thanks.' It was very dry.

'No, I mean—' She stopped abruptly.

'Don't try to explain,' he said, his voice so flat she knew it was hiding amusement. 'It will either make you sound like one of those women who are convinced only the female race can do things like cooking and cleaning and—'

She threw a napkin at him, hitting him square in the face.

He placed it carefully at the side of him, continuing with barely a pause, 'Or plain jealous at my expertise.' He eyed her thoughtfully. 'I rather suspect the latter.'

'You wish.'

'Oh, I do, Rosie, I do. I wish for all sorts of things, things that would make your hair curl.'

The heat in his eyes left her in no doubt as to what form these wishes took and she grabbed for her orange juice, swallowing it hastily. When she nerved herself to look at him again he was calmly eating his food, a twist to the firm mouth telling her he had loved every moment of the little skirmish.

Breakfast set the tone for the day. For the first time in years Rosalie found herself being looked after. They had a lazy morning in the garden with the Saturday papers, and it was Kingsley who saw to elevenses, bringing out the most delicious whipped-cream coffee and shortbread fingers to her where she sat reclining in one of Beth's deckchairs. For lunch he took her off to a nearby riverside pub, where they sat in the shade of a huge red and blue striped umbrella, drinking velvety smooth, cold draught Guinness and eating chicken in the basket, whilst watching a pair of swans teaching their new signets the tricks of the trade and marshalling them into order every now and again.

Rosalie had phoned Beth's mobile three times during the morning, and just before they had left for lunch her aunt had got back to her informing her that Jeff had a bad attack of flu but that was all. 'I feel I want to stay the night up here, though, if that's okay with you?' Beth had said anxiously. 'I just want to be with him for a while, after the shock and everything. Will you and Kingsley cope all right? There's steaks in the fridge I'd got in for tonight, and salad and baby new potatoes, and a whole stack of frozen desserts in the freezer. Don't go hungry, will you?'

There was no chance of that. After a drive in the afternoon Kingsley stopped at a cottage advertising cream teas, and the mouth-watering homemade scones brim full with jam and cream and cream cakes melted in the mouth. Kingsley won the heart of the elderly owner by asking for a second round, and by the time they left they had had the older woman's life story, including the account of the giddy affair she'd had in the war with a visiting GI. 'Spoke just like you, he did,' the rosy-cheeked, bright-eyed lady—who wasn't an inch over four feet ten inches—said confidingly to Kingsley. 'And with the accent and his charm, the local lads didn't stand a chance. Course, everyone told me it'd come to nothing, but I loved him and he loved me. No doubt about that. But he got killed, see. Just a week before the war ended. I've had three husbands since then. Divorced one and buried two but there was still no one like my Hank.'

Rosalie hadn't known whether she'd wanted to laugh or cry. The little woman was a born comic and she had known it too, regaling them with one story after another about her life, which had been a fruitful one to say the least, but there had been something in her eyes when she'd spoken about her Hank that had gripped Rosalie's heart and made it ache. It hadn't helped that as they'd been leaving the lady had grabbed Rosalie's arm, forcing her to bend her head closer to the lavender-scented little body, whereupon the woman had whispered, 'Don't you let him get away, dear; you'll regret it the rest of your life if you do. And I know. Oh, yes, I know all right.'

'What did she say to you?'

Kingsley had gone ahead and was waiting on the threshold, holding open the door for her, and as Rosalie edged through the narrow aperture with her crutches she said quietly, 'Nothing really. Just that she still misses Hank.'

He shook his head as they walked towards the car. 'That's a real shame after all these years.'

'Yes. Yes, it is.' She glanced at him as he walked beside her, so attractive he made her head spin. He smelled nice. A clean, sharp aftershave with a faint scent of lemons, she thought distractedly, suddenly aware she would remember this moment—the bright sunshine, the man at her side, the smells and colours—for the rest of her life. It produced a feeling so poignant it was physically painful.

She was getting in too deep here. Panic had her heart beating a tattoo. This seductive feeling of being enclosed in his aura, of being safe from the buffeting of the storms of life, was an illusion. At the moment he wanted her in his bed and so everything was hunky-dory. All that could change with the wind.

He opened the car door for her, taking the crutches as she lowered herself into the seat and slinging them in the back before he walked round to the driver's side. She watched him, the little old lady's words ringing in her ears. But the woman hadn't known that they were just ships passing in the night, that Kingsley wouldn't want it any other way and neither would she. *She wouldn't*, she reiterated fiercely when her heart lurched. He wanted a brief affair; she didn't even want that.

Home again, Kingsley saw to the two cats who met them on the drive as though they hadn't been fed in years and were starving. Stiff tall tails expressed feline disapproval at the lateness of the hour—eight o'clock just wasn't an acceptable dinner time in their opinion.

'Steak, salad and new potatoes okay for you?' Rosalie asked when she joined him in the kitchen after checking the answer machine for messages. 'Beth's left us well provided for.'

'Sounds great.' On the way to the cottage the evening before he had insisted on stopping at an off-licence and buying several bottles of—what was to Rosalie—frighteningly expensive wine, and now he said, 'Which wine would you prefer: red, white or *rosé*?'

'*Rosé*, please.' They'd had a bottle of Kingsley's wine the night before as well as one Beth had provided, and

she had to admit—wine connoisseur that her aunt was—
Kingsley's had had the edge. Of course he wasn't sup-
porting three children all doing their own thing at university or whatever, she qualified hastily, as though the
thought had been disloyal to her aunt in some way. 'And
while I get underway with the food, you could set the
dining table if you like,' she added. The dining room was
much more formal than the way they'd eaten breakfast,
close together at the kitchen table, with his shoulder seeming to brush against her every so often, and she needed
the distance between them—mentally as well as geo-
graphically. It might be weak and pathetic but that was
the way she felt.

'It's a beautiful evening, why not alfresco?' Kingsley
suggested lazily. 'I believe in making the most of summer.'

'If you like.' Beth's round wooden patio table was an
enormous one with eight chairs—bought in mind for when
the children and their partners descended—and again was
less cosy than the kitchen.

After opening the wine Kingsley left a glass at her elbow before wandering off. Rosalie was determined to
make the fairly plain meal as good as she could, and after
seasoning the steaks she put them under the grill on a
very low heat, and with the potatoes bubbling away she
set to work preparing the salad. The beauty of Beth being
such an accomplished cook was that she usually had every
ingredient you could imagine somewhere in the kitchen,
along with plenty of fresh vegetables and fruit.

Tomatoes, avocado, baby spinach, celeriac, apple, wal-
nuts—that should be enough. Rosalie cut and grated, and
was just mixing a creamy dressing—one of her aunt's
recipes—consisting of double cream, dry mustard, lemon
thyme, black pepper and nutmeg, the juice of an orange

and lemon, and a teaspoon of Barbados sugar, when Kingsley reappeared, dipping his finger in the mixture and licking it. 'Mmm, gorgeous.' He eyed her wickedly. 'And the dressing tastes great too.'

She couldn't help but smile, even as she said warningly, 'No tasting until I say so.'

'Promises, promises…'

He refilled their glasses before coming to stand near as she mixed a pinch of coriander and parsley with garlic butter for the potatoes once they were cooked. He gently brushed a wisp of hair from her forehead, his touch feather-light, and Rosalie felt the contact shudder through her body.

'Could you check how the steaks are doing?' Her voice was breathless and she heard it with a dart of despair. She had to get a handle on all this. The trouble was she was a bunch of contradictions where Kingsley was concerned, she admitted silently. Part of her wished she had never met him, and the other part was beginning to wonder how she had managed for so long without him in her life. And that was dangerous.

She pounded the butter to within an inch of its life before she became aware that Kingsley was looking at her thoughtfully. 'Is that better?' he asked softly.

'Is what better?' she prevaricated carefully, the tell-tale burning in her cheeks causing a feeling of acute irritation with both Kingsley and herself. Why did she have to blush so easily? It was such a give-away.

'Now you've worked off some of that excess frustration, do you feel more relaxed?' he asked with aggravating composure.

She glared at him. 'How are the steaks?'

'Well and happy and demanding to be eaten.' He

walked over to her. 'So why don't you hobble off like a good girl and sit down and I'll bring everything through?'

The glare intensified. 'I've got to drain the potatoes and—'

'I am more than capable of doing that. You've done all the hard work, now it's my turn.' He handed her her glass of wine. 'Concentrate on getting to the patio with that without spilling it, okay?' He picked up the salad bowl and then the smaller one holding the dressing. 'Vamoose, woman!'

She really couldn't do anything else. By the time she had limped through to the sitting room, which led to the patio area, Kingsley was already on his way back to the kitchen, smiling at her with an unsettling blend of amusement and softness as he passed.

She was glad he wasn't with her when she walked onto the patio because she groaned out loud. He had set a corner of the table intimately for two, two candles burning in small star-shaped crystal holders and a vase of richly perfumed white roses between them. A small scalloped tablecloth covered the area of the table they were sitting at, and he'd used Beth's best plates—white china edged with platinum—and silver cutlery.

The sky had provided its own magnificent backdrop to the scene, its dusky blue streaked with tumescent crimson and violet and enriched with bands of gold, and the scent of jasmine and honeysuckle vied with the heavy perfume of the roses to create a riot on the senses.

She stood staring for a moment or two, the soft indigo dusk beyond the table warm and fragrant, and then slowly made her way to her seat. So much for distance.

Kingsley reappeared in the next moment with the potatoes and wine, looking at her with shadowed eyes. He refilled her wineglass, which had been almost empty, before he went back to the kitchen with the plates for the steaks, but he didn't speak and neither did Rosalie. Not until he was back and sitting beside her. Then she said, 'This is the way summer evenings should always be,' raising her wineglass as she added, 'To the new hotel and the continuing success of Ward Enterprises.'

He gave a phantom of a smile as he lifted his own glass. 'To the most beautiful quantity surveyor I've ever seen and getting to know each other.'

He noticed the withdrawal in her eyes his words brought forth but he didn't comment on it, gentling his voice still further as he said, 'Let me serve you.' And then he released her gaze, reaching out and picking up the bowl holding the succulently coated potatoes.

They talked of inconsequential things as the meal progressed and within minutes Rosalie was wrapped in his easy mood. He set out to make her laugh and he succeeded, creating a lazy, relaxed atmosphere enhanced by the sleeping garden and the whispering stillness of the velvet night. The moon rose, the sky becoming a dark canopy pierced with tiny flickering lights, and the rest of the world outside the garden melted away.

It was Kingsley who cleared away the dishes, returning after a while with a board containing a selection of cheeses and crackers, and another holding green and red grapes, after they'd agreed they were too full for one of Beth's rich desserts.

He handed her a cup of coffee with thick whipped cream floating on top, similar to the one he'd made earlier in the day, but this time there was the taste of orange liqueur along with the fragrant spices.

'This is delicious,' Rosalie murmured as he sat down beside her again, one arm draped casually on the back of her chair. 'Where did you learn to make coffee like this?'

He shrugged 'I don't remember.'

She stared at him. There had been something, just the faintest something that told her he was lying. He remembered all too well. Rosalie straightened in her chair. 'It was her, wasn't it?' she said flatly. 'The woman you mentioned last night, the one where you got your fingers burnt?'

He didn't prevaricate further. 'Yes, it was.'

'Why didn't you say so?' she asked quietly.

'Because I didn't think mentioning another woman would add to the evening,' he said bluntly.

'Do you mind talking about her?'

He removed his arm from the back of her chair, settling back in his seat and folding his arms as he looked at her quizzically. 'Which means you think I do,' he observed softly. Then he shrugged. 'The answer is no, not now. Not for a long time.'

She knew it wasn't fair to ask because she wasn't prepared to reciprocate regarding Miles, but she couldn't help herself. 'What happened?' she asked quietly.

'Maria was Italian and worked at one of my father's hotels. We were in love, or so I thought. What I didn't know was that I was one of many. She liked nice things, you see, and where she had come from—in a particularly poor area of Naples—a beautiful girl could make a lot of money very quickly in the age-old way. Shocked?' he asked softly.

'No,' she lied quickly. 'Of course I'm not shocked.'

'I was.'

'So…so you finished with her?' she said carefully.

'Not exactly.' He drained the cup of coffee. 'The way I found out about all the others was when she ran off with some rich oil baron she'd forgotten to mention when we got engaged. She obviously considered him a better bet than a hotel owner's son. I'm not complaining. It was the spur I needed to take hold of the business by the throat and shake it into shape. It also taught me a salutary lesson that I've never forgotten. Women lie best when they're in the horizontal position.'

She blinked. 'Some women don't lie at all.'

He smiled, coldly. 'I told you mentioning another woman wouldn't add anything to the evening.'

'It's not mentioning *her*, it's that last statement,' she returned heatedly. 'Lumping all women under the same banner.'

'Something you would never do with regard to the male sex,' he agreed smoothly. 'Right?'

She stared at him, her face reflecting her shock, and such was the expression in the dove-grey eyes that Kingsley felt like the biggest heel in the world.

She didn't try to deny the sudden self-awareness or make excuses, thus heaping—unwittingly—coals of fire on his head. What she did say was, and in a shaking voice, 'You're right, I suppose I am guilty of the same crime, but I do have my reasons.'

This was not the finish to the day he had envisaged. Damn it. And certainly not the way to penetrate that inch-thick steel armour of hers. He didn't want to make her feel bad.

He nodded. There was nothing else he could do. 'I'm sure you have,' he said flatly.

Why was it important to make him see? Rosalie sat motionless, her head whirling. And then to her absolute amazement she found herself saying, 'My mother didn't altogether die of natural causes.' She looked at him to see his reaction.

Her mother? What the hell did her mother have to do

with any of this? They were talking about this Miles guy, weren't they? 'I don't understand,' he said evenly.

'My father…he…' She didn't know how to say it because she had never spoken it out in the whole of her life. And then she found herself telling him, clearly and almost matter-of-factly, about the night when her life had been changed for ever. How she had sat on the stairs in the dark, not daring to move, but knowing something was terribly wrong. The overwhelming sickness she'd experienced, born of fright and panic, and the vomiting. But still she hadn't moved.

When she finished speaking she looked into Kingsley's face and saw the horror there. *She shouldn't have told him*, she thought desperately. He was disgusted, repulsed…

'Hell.' It was deep in his throat. And then he reached out for her, pulling her into his arms and holding her tight as he said, 'I don't know what to say, Rosie,' and such was the tone of his voice that she relaxed against him. He wasn't disgusted, she thought tremblingly. And that was enough for now.

He held her close for some time, his hands warm and strong, and then, with one hand, he tilted back her head and made her look at him. 'I'm so sorry,' he said, sincerely and softly. 'No child should have to go through something like that.'

She swallowed hard. This was too much; it was happening too fast. She was giving too much of herself.

Something of her panic must have shown in her face because he kissed her lightly on the mouth, a nondemanding, easy kind of kiss, before lowering her into her seat as he said quietly, 'Your coffee's cold and I could do with another cup before I turn in. Won't be a minute.'

She stared after him as he left, and in spite of the heat

redolent in the air and stone slabs of the patio after the hot June day, she shivered. Kingsley was the most exciting man she had ever met, the most attractive, the funniest—oh, she could go on for ever, but he was also the most lethal. He wanted a light-hearted little affair. He'd spelled it out for her just in case there had been any doubt. He wanted to make love to her, he'd told her. And what about her? Did she want to make love with him?

She swept back the hair from her face helplessly. Yes, she did, but that only showed how crazy she was and what foolishness it had been to get involved with him thus far. She had told him something she'd never told another living soul, not even Miles. Her family—her grandparents, and her mother's sisters—had never discussed the true facts about her mother's death and her father's suicide after the one time they had spelled out for her what she had to say as a child. It had been a dark and shameful secret, something to be hidden at all costs, that was what they'd all intimated. Perhaps it hadn't been intentional, but that was what she'd grown up with. And it had added to the feeling that what had happened was in some way her fault. If she hadn't been around, if she hadn't been born, her father would have had her mother all to himself and she might still be alive.

She bit down hard on her lip, shutting her eyes tightly for a moment. Reason and logic told her to think in such a way was rubbish, that there would always have been someone for her father to be jealous of, but reason and logic didn't always hold sway when the heart was involved. But now she had finally admitted the truth about the night her mother had died and why her father had taken his own life to someone, she felt the need to talk about it with Beth. To ask more about her parents' relationship, more about them as people. It had always been such an emotive issue with her grandparents. She knew they had loved her but right until the day her grandmother had died, some seven years ago, followed by her grandfather five years later, she'd known the subject was a closed book.

She supposed in a way she had been a sitting duck for someone like Miles who liked to dominate and control. She'd been so full of self-doubt and guilt, so easily crushed...

'One coffee.' Kingsley's voice in her ear brought her out of the dark thoughts.

'Thank you.' She smiled up at him as he placed the cup in front of her and then tensed as he bent down, his lips caressing her neck before moving up to her mouth. Warmth spread through her and she no longer felt the chill of the past. Her eyelids were closed, and in the safe velvety darkness she let herself be carried along on the wave of desire, responding to the voluptuous exploring of her mouth and the slow, insistent building of sensation. He took his time, pleasuring himself as well as her, and by the time his lips left hers she was aching in her inner core and ready for more.

'Drink your coffee.' His voice was husky.

She opened her eyes as he straightened and took his seat, flushing hotly at the knowledge that he knew how completely he had aroused her. Why had he stopped? She lowered her head as thoughts tumbled about in her mind. To prove that he was the one in control, was that it? And then she chastised herself in the next instant, sipping the coffee almost without tasting it. It had been her who had insisted they progress slowly; he was only keeping to the bargain.

The kiss had left her tense and frustrated, and the former easy atmosphere had disappeared. Kingsley sat quietly, not trying to diffuse the electricity vibrating between them, and Rosalie found herself gulping down the coffee in silence, screamingly aware of the big male body just a foot or so away.

Had he kissed her like that in preparation for a big seduction line in a few minutes? she asked herself as she drained her cup. Was that it? Certainly his kisses and touch swept her away from caution, but she wasn't seriously considering sleeping with a man who didn't love her and wanted an affair without any serious commitment. *Was she?* Alarm overwhelmed her that she had had to question herself, and now she emphasised strongly, No, she wasn't. She was not.

'Why don't you go on up and I'll clear away down here?' His voice was level, cool even, and she raised startled eyes to his face, the flickering candles turning him into a monochrome of black and white in the shadows of the night.

'No, I'll help,' she said quickly.

'What's to help? There's just a few things to carry through and the dishwasher will take care of everything.'

So…no seduction scene, then? She didn't allow herself to recognise the thread of disappointment, shrugging lightly as she said, 'If you're sure?'

'Sure I'm sure.' He smiled but his eyes were searching. 'But once the plaster's off it'll be a different story. I'll expect to be waited on hand and foot then.'

'Expect all you like.' She smiled too but it was forced. He spoke as if they were going to go on seeing each other, as though this was just the beginning, and it frightened her. And thrilled her—which was even more scary.

She stood up carefully. She hadn't bothered with the crutches tonight—they were more trouble than they were worth in the house. He rose with her, reaching out for her but holding her away from him slightly as he studied her face, a half-smile curving his lips. 'You're a very complex woman,' he said softly. 'Do you know that? But I'm not complaining. I've a feeling boredom is not an option around you.'

'Is that a compliment?' She could feel the colour that had crept into her cheeks whereas he was annoyingly cool, calm and collected. But then Kingsley never gave anything away.

'What do you think?' he drawled slowly.

His hands were warm on her back, his eyes piercingly blue as they held hers, and he just looked at her, saying nothing as she searched for an adequate reply and found her brain had stalled. Which happened fairly often around him.

Surprisingly, he didn't kiss her. Instead he raised a hand to the smooth silky skin at the side of her face, stroking down one cheek as he said quietly, 'Goodnight, Rosie.'

'Goodnight.' It was a whisper, and his arms held her for one more second before she was free.

Beth and George were home in time for Beth to insist on cooking a huge Sunday lunch the next day. According to George, in a low aside to Rosalie when his wife was out of the room, Jeff was now back home in his flat and had made it clear he preferred the current girlfriend feeding him grapes and ministering to his every need, rather than his mother. 'Understandable at his age,' George had added quietly, 'but I think Beth was a bit upset. Let her spoil you today, eh?'

She had smiled back, whispering, 'A nod's as good as a wink. I'll explain things to Kingsley.'

*   *   *

After that, the first time Rosalie and Kingsley were alone again was in the car on the way back to Rosalie's flat.

'Thanks for being so nice to Beth today,' Rosalie ventured as she settled back in her seat after waving goodbye to her aunt and uncle. Kingsley had dutifully eaten everything put before him and had second and even third helpings when Beth had prompted him, played cards for part of the afternoon with the older couple although Rosalie could tell it wasn't his kind of thing, and discussed the different merits of French, Italian and Australian wine with Beth for ages—although wine definitely *was* his thing. Nevertheless, she realised he had put himself out for her aunt after she'd explained the reason for the older couple's sudden arrival back at the house; being deliberately amusing and teasing Beth until the hurt look at the back of her eyes had faded and she'd become her old self.

'It's not difficult, she's a very warm and giving lady,' he said quietly. 'She reminds me of my mother in a way.'

'Your mother?' He hadn't spoken of his parents at all. She glanced at him, the chiselled profile doing funny things to her heartbeat. Ridiculous, but she couldn't imagine him ever being child size.

He nodded. 'She died when I was twelve. She'd had a hard time having me and had been told any more babies might be fatal, but eventually she persuaded my father to try for another...' He shrugged. 'The unborn child died with her. My father married again three years later. My stepmother and I did not get on.'

'I'm sorry.' She stared at him, not knowing what to say.

He shrugged. 'It's history now. My father died when I was thirty and my stepmother has since remarried.' He glanced at her, a wry twist to his mouth. 'I was not invited to the wedding. It was a relief not to have to refuse the invitation.'

'Things were still as bad as that?'

'I can see now, looking back, that I wasn't the easiest kid in the world for her to handle. As far as I was concerned my father's interest in another woman besmirched my mother's memory and they both had to pay for the desecration, added to which she was a hard, blonde, painted bimbo with pound signs for eyes.' He shrugged. 'Believe me, I don't exaggerate.'

'Right.' She took another glance and wondered if she dared risk a quip to lighten what had suddenly become a heavy conversation. 'Don't mince words, Kingsley,' she said softly. 'Tell it as it is.'

He grinned at her, totally unabashed. 'I always do, honey,' he assured her evenly. 'I always do.'

Once they drew up outside the flat Rosalie felt she could do nothing else but invite him in for coffee, an invitation Kingsley accepted with alacrity.

Late evening sunshine was streaming in through the sitting-room windows when she opened the door, enhancing the soft buttery colour scheme and mellowing the pine furniture. 'Sit down, I won't be a moment.' She gestured to the sofa and then hobbled off to the kitchen. She had bought a small wheeled trolley since the accident and found it indispensable.

Kingsley was sitting on the thick carpet looking through her music collection when she wheeled the trolley in. 'No jazz?'

'Sorry, not my scene.'

'I can see I'm going to have to educate you in all manner of things,' he said softly.

She ignored that; it seemed appropriate when he looked so broodingly sexy. He finally decided on some classical

music she'd had for some time, and she was just beginning to relax after he had moved to sit beside her when
he said, out of the blue, 'Did I mention I'm looking for a
house in London?'

For a moment she was speechless. 'You are?' she managed at last. 'Why on earth are you doing that?'

He glanced down at her, putting his coffee-cup on the
little table at the side of the sofa and slipping an arm
comfortably round her shoulders as he said, 'It seems
more sensible than all the inconvenience of hotels.'

'But you'll have your own—hotel, I mean. Surely you
can have a suite reserved in that for your own use when
you're in England? And your main business is in the
States, isn't it?'

'At the moment,' he agreed smoothly. 'But I want to
develop the English project to include at least three more
hotel complexes over here.'

'You do?' She just didn't know how to handle that.

She hadn't realised the tone of her voice until he said,
his drawl silky but with an edge to it, 'I'd have thought
you'd be pleased. No doubt Carr and Partners will get the
business again, if the job is done right this time, of
course.'

Her throat had locked and she had to swallow twice
before she could say, 'Of course it will be done right,'
knowing she was skirting the main issue.

'In spite of the business I'm in, I've never liked staying
for any length of time in a hotel,' he continued, the hard-
ness of his thigh against hers setting up a chain reaction
Rosalie could have done without. 'On the one hand they
are impersonal, not like a home, and on the other—with
me owning the damn thing—my employees are a sight
too nosy about my comings and goings. It's like living in
a goldfish bowl at times.'

And no doubt his love life made interesting observation, she thought testily. She schooled her voice to show no expression. 'I can understand that.'

'Me not liking hotels or my staff's intrusiveness?'

She took a sip of her coffee. 'Both,' she said coolly.

She felt the blue gaze searching her face but she kept her eyes focused on the cup in her hands, and after a moment he said, 'So, any suggestions?' as he settled back, one knee over the other.

'Suggestions?' She raised fine eyebrows in bland enquiry.

'On property,' he said patiently.

'I wouldn't have a clue on the sort of thing that might interest you,' she pointed out carefully. 'Would you want a flat or a house or what?'

'Not a what.' He was smiling above her head; she could feel it. 'Probably a flat. I've got the house in New York and a villa in Jamaica, so maybe a flat would be appropriate here.'

A house and a villa? Lucky old him. Rosalie didn't know why the thought of Kingsley buying a base in London was so unsettling, but it was. Which was crazy when you thought about it. London was more than big enough to take the pair of them and make sure they never bumped into each other for the rest of their lives! She took a deep breath. 'You'd be better going to an expert,' she said pleasantly.

'Do you know, I might just do that.'

Her heart gave an unsteady thud. She should never have agreed to work for him in the first place, that way none of this would be happening. But Mike would have thrown a blue fit if he had learnt she was turning business away, especially the sort of business Kingsley represented.

Her hands tightened on the coffee-cup. No, she'd had

no choice, she reassured herself firmly. Since Jamie's dinner party events had unfurled almost of their own accord—aided and abetted by Kingsley, of course.

She glanced up at him and the blue eyes were waiting for her. 'I'd better be going. I fly back to the States first thing in the morning,' he said, the tone lazy.

'You do?' She was surprised. 'But...'

'Yes?'

'You only arrived on Friday, didn't you?'

He nodded, his eyes tight on her puzzled face.

'But surely the business you came to England about, the hotel...' She tried to get her thoughts in order. 'Don't you need to deal with it?' she asked.

His thumbs traced patterns along her cheekbones before he kissed her, very thoroughly. 'Who said I came over on business?' he murmured huskily, rising to his feet. 'Sleep tight, Rosie.'

And he left.

CHAPTER SEVEN

'SO WHEN are you seeing him again?'

It was the following night, and, lo and behold, Beth had turned up on Rosalie's doorstep as soon as she'd got in from work. Her aunt had apparently come into town to do a spot of shopping—believe that, believe anything, Rosalie thought irritably. As soon as she'd answered the door to Beth the one and only topic of conversation had been a tall, dark American, and it was clear Beth had been completely bowled over.

'I told you, I don't know.' The two women were sitting having a relaxing glass of wine whilst they waited for the pizza Rosalie had ordered to be delivered, or at least it would have been relaxing but for Beth's one-track mind.

'But you *are* going out together, officially, I mean? It's not one of these horrible modern arrangements where each party is free to do this, that or the other?' Beth asked anxiously.

'Beth—'

'Oh, it's not! Tell me it's not, Lee.'

'I can't get a word in edgeways to tell you anything.' Rosalie softened the words with a smile, but inwardly she was wondering how on earth to explain her relationship with Kingsley to Beth, when she didn't know if she was on foot or horseback herself. 'I told you how we met and that I'm doing the quantity surveying for Ward Enterprises,' she said carefully, 'and we've agreed to date a little when he's in England and see how it goes from there.' And it would go absolutely nowhere.

'So he's not going out with anyone in the States in the meantime?' Beth leant forward, her eyes on Rosalie's face.

Good question. 'I assume not,' Rosalie said even more carefully. But who knew with a man like Kingsley Ward?

Beth wriggled a little, the way she did when she wasn't totally satisfied about something. 'Lee, he's absolutely gorgeous, the most divine man since…since—' words evidently couldn't adequately express Kingsley's divinity '—since *ever*, and you haven't even set up ground rules?' Beth wailed.

'It's not like that.'

'It never *will* be like that with a man as sexy as him if you don't insist on it being so,' Beth said anxiously.

'I'm not sure I want a relationship with Kingsley.' There, she'd said it, and now she waited for the storm to burst over her head as she stared straight at her aunt.

Surprisingly Beth just slumped back in her seat before reaching across and pouring herself another glass of wine, drinking half of it before she sighed, long and loudly. 'It's him, swine face, isn't it?' Swine face had been Beth's nickname for Miles since the divorce. 'You aren't still thinking about him, are you? In any fond way, I mean?'

Funny how she had been asked that twice in as many days. 'Memories softened by time and made sentimental?' Rosalie asked evenly. 'Beth, that just doesn't apply where he was concerned.'

Beth leant forward. 'It's probably the wine talking on an empty stomach,' she said earnestly, 'but has whatever went on between you and Miles put you off trying with someone else, Lee? Because if it has, don't let it. Not now, not with Kingsley. Men like him come along once in a blue moon.'

Rosalie hesitated, and then she said, very quietly, 'Marriage to Miles was a living nightmare, Beth. You don't know the half.' She took a big gulp of the wine.

'Oh, Lee.' Beth gazed at her, her plump, pretty face tragic.

Rosalie took a deep breath. 'I know the family don't like to talk about my mother and father, but compared to Miles my father was positively normal.'

Beth stared at her. 'It's not that we, me and George, don't want to talk about your parents, but we thought *you* didn't want to. You never have.'

'Because it was always an absolute taboo. I thought you were all too ashamed of what had happened.'

'No, no.' Beth was clearly horrified. 'But Mum and Dad, all of us, weren't sure of how much you actually saw and what you remembered, you were only a little dot after all, and Mum thought if we didn't harp on you'd get over everything quicker.'

'Oh, Beth.' Rosalie shook her head slowly, and then as she began to talk it all came out. All the doubts and fears and shame and guilt that had been shut away in her head for so many years, and the more she talked, the more Beth responded until the pair of them were crying on each other. But the tears were healthy and cleansing.

'Your father adored you, Lee,' Beth said at one point. 'Never think otherwise. We all used to say how strange it was that he was never jealous of you in spite of the way your mother loved you, whereas the rest of us… We had a job to get over the threshold. But he looked on you as an extension of himself and your mother, I think. That was the thing.'

Rosalie felt like a great weight had been lifted off her shoulders. 'What made you mention your mum and dad like that tonight anyway?' Beth asked suddenly.

Now it was Rosalie's turn to wriggle a little. 'I was

talking to Kingsley about them at the weekend,' she admitted.

'Ah, yes, Kingsley. Where had we got to on that subject?' Beth said immediately, homing in with the single-mindedness that often caused her offspring to turn tail and run.

'Leave it, Beth.' Rosalie eyed her aunt warningly.

'Oh, yes. You aren't sure if you want a relationship with the most gorgeous thing on two legs ever likely to hit these shores. Right?' Beth went on as though she hadn't heard.

Rosalie's gaze held more than a little exasperation. 'It's not like that,' she said firmly. 'We're—' what were they? '—friends.' It sounded incredibly weak, even to her.

Beth opened her mouth but whatever protest she was going to make was cut off by the buzzer to Rosalie's flat. Beth jumped to her feet. 'The pizza guy.' Beth jumped to her feet. 'I'll get it.'

Rosalie had pulled herself to her feet and was on her way to the kitchen when she was stopped in her tracks in the doorway to the sitting room by the sight of Beth almost buried under a mountain of flowers. The bouquet of tiger lilies and creamy pale orchids wasn't the average red-roses type of declaration of a man to a woman, but then Kingsley wasn't the average man.

Beth was clearly thinking the same thing because there was a significant little silence as the older woman gave the younger a long, meaningful look before she said, 'Friends...right.'

Rosalie counted silently to ten. 'That's all, Beth,' she said brightly, 'and who's to say these flowers are from Kingsley anyway?' As if there could be the faintest chance they weren't!

'You mean you've more than one gorgeous man after

you? No one could be that lucky.' Beth mirrored Rosalie's thoughts.

They were from Kingsley. The card simply said, 'Thinking of you, K'. Which was utterly Kingsley.

When the pizza finally arrived Beth bustled about sharing it out onto the plates Rosalie had got ready, carrying two trays through to the sitting room where they'd planned to eat watching their favourite soap on TV. In the meantime Rosalie arranged the flowers in two big heavy vases and then left them standing on the work surface in the kitchen. She'd bring them through to the sitting room when her aunt had gone, she thought flatly, otherwise they'd act as a spur to keep Beth twittering on about Kingsley all evening.

Her eyes returned to the card just before she left the kitchen. 'Thinking about you.' No kisses, no cloying message that dripped sentiment. Simply 'thinking about you'. Was he? His life was as far removed from hers as the man in the moon. Had he given her more than a passing thought since he'd left? Flowers were easy. Miles had bought her a bunch every day for weeks when they had first got together, sending the girls in her block at the university green with envy, but after she had left him she'd discovered that even then he had been messing about with other women.

She clicked her tongue irritably, annoyed with herself for both dredging up the past and allowing such cynicism to spoil what should have been rather a nice moment. They were unquestionably fabulous, the flowers…

Beth's taxi came just after nine and Rosalie decided to have a long hot soak in the tub with some wildly expensive bath oil she'd had for Christmas, and pamper herself a little. She took the remainder of her glass of wine through with her, lighting a couple of perfumed candles and turning off the main light so she could relax in the flickering candlelight.

She had long since stopped feeling slightly ridiculous due to having to wedge the plastered foot on the chrome bath rack that fitted across the bath, and now as she lay carefully back in the silky water she shut her eyes, sighing softly and contentedly. The sensuous warmth and evocative perfume emptied her mind of everything but the moment, and she felt the tension flowing out of her in a relaxing wave.

And then the telephone rang. And rang. And rang. When she couldn't ignore it a moment longer she hoisted herself out of the water, grumbling profusely, and warning of dire consequences should it stop the second before she reached it. Grabbing a bath towel, she shuffled out into the vibrating hall.

'*Hello?*' She had barked into the receiver, which wasn't her normal telephone manner at all.

There was a moment of startled silence, and then, 'Rosie? Is that you?' a deep, unmistakable voice said with some surprise.

'Kingsley?' Her voice was high and she fought to moderate it when she said a little breathlessly, 'I thought you were in the States?'

'I am.' She could tell he was smiling. 'Did you get the flowers?' The smoky tone to his voice curled her toes.

'The flowers? Oh, yes, yes, they're wonderful. Thank you.' *Pull yourself together, for crying out loud.* She was babbling like an idiot. 'What...what time is it there?'

'The time doesn't matter.' His voice was deep, husky, as clear as if he were in the next room, and Rosalie shivered, though not from cold. 'Had a good day?' he asked softly.

'Fine.' Her heart was thumping so hard she put her

hand on her chest before she could manage to say, 'And you?'

'So-so.' A slight pause. 'I've been dreaming of you, whether I'm awake or asleep. What do you think that means?'

She swallowed hard. Keep it light, Rosalie. 'You've eaten too much cheese?' she suggested levelly.

He chuckled and her heart turned right over. 'I wanted to hear your voice,' he admitted quietly. 'Right now, this minute. Crazy, eh? What have you done to me?'

She swallowed again, feeling the drips of water trickling down her skin where the towel wasn't touching.

'It was a good weekend,' he murmured. 'The best I've had in a long, long time. Thank Beth and George again for me when you speak to them. They're real nice people.'

'Beth's just left.' Her stomach was curling at the tone of his voice, its seductive quality mesmerising, and to combat the feeling she added, 'Utterly blown away by the flowers, incidentally. You'd have thought she'd received them herself.'

'I've sent her some, as it happens, a basket of freesias.'

'You have? That's kind of you,' she said carefully.

There was the briefest of pauses, and then his voice held a velvet touch when he said, 'And you're quite right in thinking it's a ploy to inveigle my way further into her good books. I've a feeling I'm going to need every weapon at my disposal where you're concerned.' It was totally unapologetic.

Rosalie blinked, a curious rush of exhilaration causing her to shut her eyes tightly for a second. 'What Beth thinks or doesn't think is neither here or there,' she said as severely as she could considering a big grin was trying to make itself felt. 'I'm my own woman.' Or had been before she'd met him.

'You wouldn't be so mean as to hold onto every little bit, surely? There's enough to go round for a starving man.'

'Are you saying I'm fat?' she said lightly, a part of her mind hearing herself flirting with amazement.

'You're perfect. For me, that is,' he said huskily.

Help. She was too rusty at this game to survive for more than a moment. Her thought process hiccuped and died.

'Rosie? Are you still there?'

'Yes.' Pull yourself together, act nonchalant and cool as though this isn't blowing you away.

'Look, I've got to go, there's a problem at one of the hotel sites here—some flooding. I was hoping to be back in England at the weekend but it's beginning to look as though it might be longer before I can get away.'

She took a deep breath. 'That's all right,' she said briskly. 'If there's any complications or difficulties with the job here, I've got numbers I can call, and your architect is very helpful.'

'Damn my architect,' he said levelly. 'I want to hold you, to kiss you, to—' Another pause and then he said, his voice dry, 'Goodnight, Rosie. Sweet dreams…as long as they're of me.'

'Goodnight.' She replaced the receiver in something of a daze.

Once Rosalie was back in the bath she found all thoughts of peaceful contemplation had been blown out of the water by Kingsley's voice. Just hearing the smoky tones had evoked all sorts of emotions, and not one of them sensible or sane.

She spent the rest of her time in the bathroom giving herself a severe talking-to. She was a modern career woman who had her sights set on advancement, and she'd

already come a long way in the last ten years. Relationships—*any* relationships—meant give and take, and it was
the law of dynamics that one partner would take more
than the other. Control and manipulation weren't far behind then. And Kingsley was the type of man whose
whole life had been built on the will to control, ever since
his broken engagement anyway. He'd said himself that
he'd carved his empire from a desire to reach out and take
life by the throat and choke it into submission.

But all that aside, forgetting all she knew about the
motivation that drove him and his cold-blooded attitude
to affairs of the heart, it was her own feelings where
Kingsley was concerned that told her it would be emotional suicide to get involved with him, even slightly. For
some reason he had got under her skin, and, much as she
would like to lie to herself and say it was just a physical
attraction and easily dealt with, the weekend had shown
her differently. She enjoyed being with him too much; she
liked him too much.

Miles had swept her off her feet and into his arms, and
she had married him in a fever of love and physical desire
without knowing the real person beneath the façade. He
had fooled her and she'd paid the price.

Kingsley wasn't like that. He had shown himself in his
true colours from day one. Offended as she'd been, he
had stated he would never fall in love with her and wanted
an affair he could walk away from with no complications
or messy feelings to complicate the nice clean finish.

She levered herself out of the bath, staring at her reflection in the misted mirror for a moment or two. She
couldn't turn her feelings off and on at will, much as she
would like to right at this minute. Neither did she want
to put herself in a position where a man had the power to
bring her to her knees again, and she had the feeling that,

much as Miles had hurt her, Kingsley could hurt her a thousand times more. She'd survived devastation once and at least she hadn't brought it on herself knowingly. If she got involved with Kingsley she wouldn't have that comfort when it all went wrong.

She went to bed that night determined she was not going to agonise any further over Kingsley. It was simple, quite simple when you considered all the facts logically, that she would be crazy to let their association grow stronger. He had said they would take it as slowly as she liked. Fine. Then it *would* be slow, so slow a virile, red-blooded man like Kingsley would soon lose interest and move on to pastures new.

She would keep busy at work, go out with some of her girlfriends on a more regular basis and start letting her hair down a bit, book a sumptuous holiday somewhere for next year and generally revamp her life. Perhaps meeting Kingsley had done her a favour after all, motivating her to take stock and decide what she really wanted out of life? She nodded firmly, turning over and almost immediately falling asleep.

But the subconscious wasn't so easily conquered. In her sleep Rosalie was vulnerable to the ghosts she kept under lock and key most of the time during the day, and, probably because of the weekend and then Kingsley's phone call, she found herself in a deep, dark valley of shifting shadows and half-recognisable images, past and present interweaving.

She awoke some time in the middle of the night when it was still dark, tears running down her face and her whole body tense with the nightmare. Kingsley had been there, but a different Kingsley, one who had brown eyes and not blue, and who had been crimson with anger, shouting, hitting, punching…

She sat up in bed, aware her nightie was clinging to her damp body, and ran a shaking hand over her face, brushing back the hair sticking to her wet cheeks.

Why hadn't she left Miles long before their graduation night? It was a question she had asked herself many times. But she had been so much younger then, so confused and frightened. She had got used to him hitting her when he was in one of his moods, even punching her on occasion, but he had always been so sorry later she had forgiven him. He was Miles Stuart—the man everyone said she was so lucky to have married—so their rows *had* to be her fault.

And then that night, after they had partied with their friends and most people had drunk too much, she'd inadvertently walked into one of the bedrooms at the big house the party was being held in, thinking it was the bathroom. Miles and one of their friends had been in bed together.

She had shouted and stormed out of the house, intending to walk home to the flat they'd rented, and Miles had come after her in his sports car. She had actually thought he'd come to plead with her when she'd heard the car engine, but he had got out and hit her so hard she'd been dazed and barely conscious. He'd bundled her into the front seat and driven home, and there he had attacked her again. But that night the worm had turned.

Rosalie closed her eyes, hugging her knees to her chest as the past rose up on the screen in her mind. It had been a night that had finally killed the last remnant of love for him.

When Miles had begun punching her this time something had snapped and she'd fought back, kicking and scratching and biting for all she was worth. Quite when she had realised he'd intended to rape her she didn't know, but it had only been one of their neighbours kicking the front door in that had saved her, and that at the last moment.

The divorce had been quick and silent, Miles's parents had made sure of that once they had seen the evidence stacked against their son. They had been petrified she'd drag the family name through the mud along with Miles, and she would have. Oh, yes, she would have if he hadn't met all her requirements, even though it would have crucified her to reveal the facts of their marriage to anyone other than her kindly solicitor.

She could still remember how she had felt the moment she had finally and legally been free of him. She'd been physically and mentally exhausted the weeks leading up to the divorce, but on that day it had been as though an invisible weight, which had kept her mind and limbs leaden and dull, had been lifted off her body and she had felt as light as a bird. It hadn't lasted, of course—grim reality had had to be faced and she'd found the memories of the abuse and torment she'd suffered at Miles's hands reared up at the oddest moments, but always there was the recollection of that moment when her soul had soared.

Rosalie took a deep breath, slipping out of bed and padding across to the chest of drawers where she found a clean hanky and blew her nose unelegantly.

People went through far worse than her, she told herself firmly. She hadn't been disfigured or disabled in an accident or lost a child; she wasn't friendless or starving or living on the streets. She had a lovely home and a fulfilling job, and normally she was perfectly happy. Everything had only begun to go pear-shaped since Kingsley had appeared on the scene. Once he left she'd be fine.

She ignored the lurch her stomach gave at the idea of

a life in which Kingsley didn't feature, and snuggled under the covers again.

Mind over matter, she thought with determination, that was what all this was about. Hearing his voice so unexpectedly tonight had caused a little blip in the process, but she could cope with that. She had to distance herself from Kingsley Ward in her head and her body would follow suit. Simple, really…

CHAPTER EIGHT

SUMMER was in full bloom, and London was in the grip of a heatwave that sent hordes of office workers flocking to the capital's parks in their lunch hours, where they ate their sandwiches under leafy trees and grumbled about having to return to work in such beautiful weather.

All Rosalie was concerned about was the fact that the plaster was off, her ankle had mended well and the itching that had sent her crazy the last few days was gone.

It had been two weeks since the weekend with Kingsley at Beth's, and he had not been back in the country since then although he had phoned Rosalie several times. Each time he did she promised herself that the next time she wouldn't be breathless and shivery and excited. But then broken promises to yourself didn't count.

On the fifteenth day she had yet another call, this time at work. He was arriving at Heathrow around sixish, Kingsley drawled easily, his voice deep and smoky. He'd like to do dinner if she was available? He'd pick her up at eight and they could go to a club he knew, somewhere where the food was good and they could dance a little to celebrate the plaster coming off. How did that sound?

This was the perfect opportunity to slow things right down, Rosalie told herself silently. They hadn't seen each other in a while, and putting a date off would send a message even Kingsley's ego couldn't ignore. She could be pleasant but cool.

'Dinner?' She took a steadying breath. 'I'd love to.'

'Great.' His voice was warm and it caused her skin to tingle.

No, not great. Stupid, stupid, stupid!

There was a pause, and then he said very softly, 'Have you been good whilst I've been gone?'

Okay, you've already let the side down once, don't compound it by going all weak and fluttery just because his voice is reaching the parts no one else's could. 'Good? Well, I've shared my favours equally between all my many lovers, so would you say that's being good?' she said lightly, eternally thankful he couldn't see her flushed face and trembling hands. 'How about you?' she added, careful to keep her voice matter-of-fact.

'All work and no play isn't what it's cut out to be,' he said wryly. 'Not by a long chalk.'

Rosalie swallowed; the sensual quivers stirring her blood were drying her mouth too. She forced herself to say just as lightly as before, 'That's because you haven't had any practice in the art of denial, perhaps?' allowing a little sting in her tone.

'Perhaps. So, do I get a reward for being good?'

'Being good is its own reward,' she said primly.

'Like hell it is. I'll see you at eight. Bye, Rosie.'

She stared at the phone for a few moments before replacing the receiver, shaking her head as she did so. Mad, that was what she was. Stark staring mad.

Ten to eight that evening found Rosalie outwardly poised and perfectly groomed, but inwardly shaking. It was when she caught herself agitatedly pacing the sitting room that she warned herself to calm down. She wandered through to the bedroom again, checking her appearance in the long thin mirror to one side of the bed as though she hadn't already stood there for a long time already.

She had put her hair up for the first time in ages and now her slender neck was revealed by the upswept hairstyle, her eyes with their touch of eyeshadow and mascara seeming extra big and the scarlet gloss lipstick giving a touch of sophistication her confidence desperately needed.

The one-shouldered muslin and satin cocktail dress that ended just below her knees shouldn't have been her colour in deep scarlet, but it actually brought out the richness in her hair without clashing with the chestnut tones, and she had teamed it with simple strappy charcoal-grey sandals and clutch bag.

It had been thanks to Beth that she had tried the dress on some months earlier in one of the fashionable boutiques. Normally she wouldn't have touched the colour, but once on the dress had looked a million dollars—as it should have for the price! However, at the last moment she had chickened out of wearing it for the evening with the other partners and their wives and the rest of the staff at Carr and Partners' Christmas party, deciding it clung just a little too provocatively in places. But tonight... tonight the dress's unquestionable elegance and the way it transformed her figure into an hourglass was just what she needed.

When the buzzer sounded she counted to ten and then spoke into the little box on her hall wall. 'Yes?'

'It's Kingsley.'

Her heart thudded. She pressed the release for the house's front door and then opened the door of the flat, meeting him in the hall.

'Wow.' He smiled, and before she could say a word he was kissing her. It was a warm, confident kiss, a kiss that stated he had a perfect right to hold her and that he knew she would accept his embrace, but he didn't prolong the caress, raising his head as he released her and stepped back a pace. 'You look like all my dreams rolled into one,' he said lazily, with the touch of mockery she remembered.

'All of them?' she said smilingly, hoping he couldn't sense what the kiss had done to her equilibrium. 'Blonde, red and brunette ones?'

He didn't say anything for a second, but then one of his hands touched her hair. 'I only dream warm brown with tones of red these days.' His eyes moved over her face. 'And grey eyes, small nose, full, kissable lips. Mmm, very kissable lips…'

She stopped him with an upraised hand as he went to take her into his arms again, laughing as she said, 'I hate to tell you, but these kissable lips have left lipstick on yours. Unless you want to be thought of as a very modern man I suggest you wipe it off before we go out.'

He took her arm, gently moving her into her hall and closing the flat door before he said, 'One thing at a time…'

This time the kiss lasted longer and was more intimate, his arms moulding her body into his and his lips firm and warm as they took what they wanted. Rosalie was aware she was kissing him back and that it would be giving him all the wrong signals, but she couldn't help it, she told herself feverishly. He only had to touch her and she seemed to melt and lose all reason.

Not that that was any excuse, she admitted honestly in the next second when she was free again, but it was the truth none the less.

'I'll need to do my lipstick again.' She took a backward step as she spoke as though she thought he was going to reach for her again, her cheeks pink.

'Sure,' he said softly, his eyes laughing at her as he took out a crisp white handkerchief and began to wipe the scarlet from his mouth. 'Go ahead. I'm not going any-where.'

Once in the taxi—which had been clocking up the kiss-ing time—he took her hand, asking her about her day and telling her about his, and what had been happening the last couple of weeks. They continued with the same kind of easy inconsequential conversation once they got to the nightclub, a lush affair with a very good jazz band and a dance floor that demanded closeness.

Their table was in a nice spot—not so near the band that they were deafened, but close to the dance floor—and after Kingsley had ordered a bottle of champagne he leant back in his seat, the bright blueness of his eyes hold-ing hers. 'I'm glad the ankle mended so well,' he said quietly. 'We can do this more often now.' His eyes chal-lenged her to disagree.

She stared at him, aware that the hint of intimacy that had been hanging in the air between them since the kiss in the hall was stronger than ever. 'As often as your busy life and mine allows,' she said at last, aiming to make it casual but knowing she hadn't responded quickly enough for that. 'Which won't be all that much, I suppose.'

He gave her a long, silent look. 'Then we'll have to make sure it is, won't we?' He shifted in his chair and every nerve in her body registered the movement. 'Friends should see each other often,' he drawled with lazy mock-ery.

Friends? She didn't know how to take that.

He was watching her with a kind of amused specula-tion, his lips curving just the slightest. He knew just how he affected her. She shrugged carefully just as the waiter appeared with the champagne, and once he had gone and she was sipping her glass of frothy bubbles Kingsley leant forward, all amusement gone. 'I like you very much,

Rosie,' he said huskily. 'It's important you know that. I didn't like the way you were on my mind at first, but then…then I welcomed it. I don't want to rush you, I still hold to that, but the way I feel about you…' One finger touched her mouth, slowly outlining her lips.

What was he saying? She took a big gulp of champagne. She didn't know where she was with this man from one moment to the next. One minute intense, the next mocking. Chameleon man.

He had sat back in his seat again as she had reached for her glass, and now he said quietly, 'Does that bother you?' He was watching her very closely.

Her smile was brittle. 'Of course not. Everyone likes to be liked, don't they?' A strange feeling was taking hold of her, uncertainty telling her she would be faintly relieved if he was still talking about just an affair and nothing more. But only faintly. Which was more crazy than anything that had gone before. A man like Kingsley wasn't for her. She knew that.

'I don't know,' he said levelly. 'You tell me.'

'There's no harm in liking.' She shrugged offhandedly.

'And if liking grows to something more?' he pressed softly.

She blinked, tearing her eyes away from his. She tried to think of something to say to bring the conversation back to normality and failed utterly.

'I see.' His voice was very soft, very deep.

Her heart quickened, her uneasiness transparent. 'What do you see?' she asked boldly, because she really wanted to know.

He didn't answer that. What he did say was, and still very softly, 'We've a long way to go, haven't we?' It was a statement, not a question. He observed her in silence, waiting.

A different waiter appeared with two menus, and Rosalie was so pleased to see him she could have kissed him. She took hers with such effusive thanks the poor man backed away with something like alarm on his face.

When he had gone with a promise to return in a few minutes, Kingsley took the menu out of her hands, his touch very gentle. He lifted her chin, forcing her eyes to meet piercing blue, and then he said, 'You told me about your mother and father, Rosie, can't you tell me about him?'

'No.' One word, but blatant in what it conveyed.

He gave her a long, searching look. 'Okay.' He released her, picking up her menu and placing it in her nerveless fingers. 'I'd recommend something but as it would mean you eating something else I won't try that one again,' he said pleasantly.

She glanced at him, relieved when he smiled at her. 'That was stupid,' she admitted weakly, feeling he deserved some sort of apology. 'But at the time you seemed so arrogant.'

'And now?' he asked with silky intent.

Oh, but he was good, he was very, very good, Rosalie thought helplessly. Didn't miss an opportunity, did he? But then that was undoubtedly one of the attributes that had made him such a formidable adversary in the business world. 'Now you still seem arrogant,' she said with a faint smile, 'but perhaps I'm getting used to it.' She raised mocking eyebrows, pleased with herself.

He grinned wickedly. 'There is so much more you could get used to, believe me.'

Rosalie floundered. You couldn't argue with some things.

Whether it was the champagne, or the fact that she was all dressed up and with the most gorgeous, fascinating man in the whole place, or simply that she'd had enough soul-searching for one night, Rosalie didn't know, but she found she enjoyed the rest of the evening. Kingsley had performed another chameleon manoeuvre, and turned into a perfectly charming, relaxed social animal with nothing more pressing on his mind than making the evening a good one for both of them.

The fact that this heightened the impact of his sex appeal considerably did cause her the odd problem, especially when they were dancing. He made sure she became acquainted with every inch of his undeniably powerful body, and more than once as she tottered back to her seat she wondered if other men could turn an ordinary dance into an experience of such epicurean intimacy.

He didn't realise the effect he was having on her, she was sure, but, held closely in his arms with the delicious male scent of him teasing her nostrils, she lost the rhythm more than once, excusing herself by blaming her faltering steps on her weak ankle rather than the weakness within.

It was very late when he took her home, sitting with her tucked into his side in the taxi, his arm round her and her head resting on his shoulder.

As they neared the flat the intoxicating effects of the dancing and champagne faded rapidly. She wanted to ask him in, she admitted silently, and not just for a nightcap. Could she handle what would inevitably follow? The sane, logical part of her brain told her she wouldn't be able to give him her body without giving her heart also; the other part, the part that cried out for tenderness and comfort and love, said why carry on being alone when she could be in his arms?

When the taxi drew up outside the flat Kingsley opened the door and helped her out, before leaning down and speaking to the driver through the passenger window, asking him to wait.

He wasn't coming in. Her heart thumped wildly and she honestly couldn't say if she was relieved or disappointed. Perhaps it was a mixture of both.

He took her arm and walked her to the door, standing with her on the top step as she opened it. As she went to say goodnight he pushed her inside, taking her in his arms and kissing her fiercely, without any restraint in the shadowed darkness. The taste, the smell of him spun in her head and she clung to him, running her hands over his hard body under his suit jacket, the soft silk of his shirt at odds with the hard muscles beneath.

His hands were exploring her curves, the delicate fabric of her dress doing nothing to hide the arousal evident in the peaked tips of her breasts, but although his mouth was urgent and hungry she sensed he was fully in control of himself and curiously she wished he weren't. If he got swept away by desire, taking the decision and the will to resist out of her hands, it would be *fait accompli*. She wouldn't have to think about things any more, she could just go with the flow.

And then she felt him very gently remove her from him, his hand stroking a wisp of hair from her face as though to soften the withdrawal. 'I have to go.'

She could tell him she wanted him to stay and make love to her, tell him to pay the taxi off and come back to her. 'Yes, I know.' She clenched her hands to avoid reaching out for him.

'I'll call you,' he murmured huskily. 'Okay?'

'All right.' She stared at him, her eyes huge.

He kissed her once more, and she had to restrain herself from pressing into him again, the feeling that she couldn't get close enough overpowering. Something was happening, something she had no control over and it was scary.

He touched her cheek in farewell and then opened the door fully, walking towards the taxi as she stood at the top of the steps watching him, her face as pale as alabaster. The night was almost silent except for the sound of the odd car beyond the end of the street, and just past the house a street lamp cast a circle of muted gold on the pavement. She didn't think she had ever felt so alone in all her life.

He turned and raised his hand before stepping into the taxi and she raised hers briefly in reply, letting it fall limply to her side as the taxi drew away. She watched it until it turned the corner and was lost to sight, but even then she didn't shut the door, but continued to stare out into the empty street. She wanted to cry and she didn't understand why.

Two small pinpoints of amber light shone further down the pavement as a cat sauntered out from the side of a house, a big apricot tom following a moment later.

Rosalie watched the first cat, a small dainty tabby, sashaying along in front of her beau, hips swinging and tail provocatively swaying. She fancied she could almost see the cat's eyelashes fluttering as it moved its head slightly at one point to make sure her admirer was still following.

'It's easy for you,' she murmured softly. 'No worries, no wondering if he'll still want you in the morning, no promises of for ever...'

She stepped inside and shut the door. She was beginning to talk to cats now, and ones that were out of earshot at that. The next stage was the men in white coats. Something told her it was time for bed!

That evening set the tone for plenty more in the following weeks whilst Kingsley was in England, along with long weekends when they walked in Hyde Park or took a boat on the Thames, went for champagne and strawberry picnics, visited Beth and George for enormous Sunday lunches, and generally enjoyed each other's company.

The hot spell held, and soon the newspapers were talking of hosepipe bans and water shortages, but the parks were full of happy, rosy children and tanned young mothers in short summer dresses, and everyone seemed to be smiling all the time. Including Rosalie. She kept warning herself it couldn't last, of course—the seductively so-far-and-no-further affair with Kingsley as well as the weather—but it was almost as though she was in a state of suspended animation about it all now.

She knew Kingsley wanted more from her, and she was beginning to suspect it wasn't just sexually but in all sorts of ways, but every time she asked herself what she would do if that proved the case she felt so confused she put the subject on ice.

She had known Miles for five months before she had married him, and on her wedding day she would have sworn her new husband would hold no surprises for her, except in the nicest possible way. She'd known Kingsley for less, but several times recently she had caught herself making judgements—and all of them good—about him, which just showed the old adage of once bitten, twice shy didn't always follow.

She did wonder if Kingsley might be biding his time about what he saw as the next stage of their relationship until she finished working on his hotel project. Sleeping with the quantity surveyor might not be his style, she thought wryly. He was the sort of man who would rarely mix business with pleasure, preferring to keep the different compartments of his life separate and straightforward.

Nevertheless, she had to admit to a feeling of surprise that he hadn't put pressure on her. Sometimes he kissed her with such fierce passion it stunned her, other times he was warm and tender, leaving her feeling cherished and desirable, and always wanting more. Always. Which might be a very clever strategy on his part? If he softened her up into accepting his terms he couldn't very well lose.

But in spite of debating the matter daily in her mind, and touching on all the reasons and rationalisations why she had to finish the relationship sooner rather than later, she always told herself one more date wouldn't hurt. And so it continued.

On a hot Saturday morning towards the end of July Beth arrived on her doorstep, and Rosalie knew the moment she opened the door something was afoot. She had some wonderful news, Beth announced in a flat voice. George had been offered a marvellous position in a top university in New Zealand, and with the children off their hands he felt it was the right job at the right time. It would mean moving there lock, stock and barrel, of course.

At which point Beth broke down in floods of tears. On the one hand she wanted to go, she sobbed; she certainly didn't want to hold George back and spoil things for him, and of anywhere in the world New Zealand was the one place she'd always had a hankering for, but on the other hand it would mean leaving everyone she knew and being faced with a new life in her middle age. Should they go? What did Rosalie think?

Rosalie hugged her and sat her down with a large slice of chocolate cake and a mug of coffee, and by the time Beth left an hour or so later she was brighter and seeing the positive side to the move more. Which was a good sign.

They *would* go to New Zealand, Rosalie thought, waving her aunt goodbye from the doorstep as Beth smiled at her from the taxi. And with Beth's ability to collect friends round her like moths to a flame, she'd soon find her feet. But Rosalie would miss her aunt terribly. Beth meant more to her than she'd realised.

She closed the door, wandering back inside and staring at the pile of work she'd brought home from the office the night before. Kingsley, in consultation with his architect, had accepted one of the tenders, and a builder had been engaged and had started work. Because it was such a big job various subcontractors were involved and she was visiting the site on a regular basis now, but she had other work that needed progressing for other clients, and there didn't seem enough hours in the day the last few weeks. Possibly because she was spending a large part of her free time with Kingsley, time that had been taken up with work previously.

She frowned as she collected up the empty plates and mugs, taking them through to the kitchen where she made herself another cup of coffee before starting work again.

Twenty minutes later there was another ring at the doorbell. 'Yes?' She spoke resignedly into the intercom. It was going to be one of those days where the world and his wife called, she could feel it. She was going to see a show in the West End with Kingsley tonight and they were having dinner first, so she had wanted to put in some good solid hours of work whilst she could. She needed to keep on top of things for her peace of mind.

'It's Kingsley, Rosie. I need to talk to you.'

When she opened the front door she was surprised to see him holding a suitcase. 'Is something wrong?' she asked quickly.

He nodded before kissing her, a perfunctory kiss that

nevertheless sent needles of sensation to her nerves. 'I need to fly to Jamaica urgently,' he said quietly, 'so I'm afraid tonight's off.'

She forced down her disappointment. 'Problem with a hotel?'

He shook his head. 'The friend I was best man to recently, Alex, has been involved in an accident,' he said briefly. 'Broken his neck jet-skiing. They aren't sure how bad it is and he's stuck in this hospital in Jamaica where they were honeymooning. I've known his wife as long as I've known Alex and she's got no family, poor kid. She phoned last night, hysterical, so I said I'd fly out today.'

'How awful.' She stared at him aghast.

'It was their last day there too, would you believe? He made the mistake of drinking at a party some friends they'd made threw to see them off, and then having a last ride round the bay before they changed to get ready to leave.' He shook his head. 'Damn fool,' he muttered hoarsely.

'I'm so sorry, Kingsley.' She could see he was struggling and she didn't know what else to say.

'Alex and his family were always there for me when Dad remarried; they helped me through a bad time.'

She had drawn him into the sitting room now, sitting beside him on the sofa and taking his hand as he talked.

'He's a nice guy, Rosie, you'd like him, and he lives for sport. Any kind, any place, it's a long-standing joke. It would be better for him to go straight away than be left paralysed. He wouldn't be able to handle it.'

'It might not come to that.' She squeezed his hand gently. 'Lots of people get better from such things. It just depends where the break is and what damage has been done.'

'I guess.' He sank back on the sofa, rubbing a hand

wearily over his face. 'Joanna phoned at one in the morning and I couldn't get off to sleep again. Hell, I can't believe he could be so damn stupid; he knows better than that.'

'What time do you leave?' she asked softly.

'In a couple of hours.' He stretched tiredly.

'Have you eaten?' And when he shook his head, 'Then first thing is a cup of coffee and then I'll cook us some brunch, okay?'

'Thanks,' he murmured, stopping her when she would have risen and putting a hand to her cheek, his touch so light it was like the brush of a leaf. 'I don't want to leave you,' he said huskily. 'Not like this.'

Suddenly it wasn't a time for pretending. 'I don't want you to go,' she whispered back.

He ran his fingers over her lips, outlining her mouth, and then down to her throat where he caressed the smooth silky skin delicately before pulling her into him. And then his mouth was coaxing hers open, sensation shooting to every part of her body as his lips and tongue explored hers, the hard pressure of his body as he slid her down beneath him intoxicating.

He kissed her until she was almost mindless with pleasure, his hands stroking and teasing her body as his lips plundered hers, and she knew she was trembling uncontrollably at the need he was drawing forth so effortlessly. He had kissed and caressed her many times over the last months, but never like this. Never like this.

She knew now, and in fact she had known it for weeks, that she'd been waiting for this time from the first moment she had laid eyes on him. It had been there between them, unspoken but alive and electric, the knowledge of how good they would be together.

Her breathing was coming in short pants and her breasts

felt tight and sensitive, her whole body sensitised. The will to think or hold back was gone, burnt up in the restless urgency that had surfaced under his lovemaking. She clung to him, responsive to his every demand, overwhelmed by a primitive yearning.

'You're beautiful, Rosie, so beautiful.' His lips were warm on her throat as he traced burning kisses over her skin. 'Inside and out. And you don't seem to realise it. I find that amazing.' He raised himself slightly, looking into her flushed face as he said again, 'So beautiful.'

She opened her eyes, staring into glittering blue made almost black with desire.

'I don't want an affair with you,' he murmured, his body as hard as a rock. 'I want more than that. I've fallen in love with you, Rosie. I've been fighting it since the first time I kissed you and I knew it deep inside, but I was hoping you would prove me wrong. That you would say or do something that showed me the image I had of you wasn't real. But it is.'

She had frozen in his arms, her eyes wide. This wasn't how it should be. Kingsley was a 'no complications, love 'em and leave 'em' type of guy, he'd *said* so.

'Don't you believe me?' he said softly, becoming aware of her reaction. 'Don't you, Rosie?'

Her voice was a long time in coming, and then it was a whisper when she said, 'I don't know.'

For a long moment he studied her face, his blue eyes searching hers with their penetrating light, and then he straightened up and away from her, pulling her into a sitting position at the side of him. 'You don't feel the same,' he said flatly. 'Is that it?'

She swallowed but she couldn't look at him. 'I don't know how I feel,' she said on a deep shuddering breath. 'This…this has all happened so suddenly.'

'Not from where I'm sitting.' There was a touch of wryness in his voice now. 'In the past I've wined and dined and bedded them a hundred times over by now.'

'Then...then how do you know you feel differently about me to all the others?' she managed. 'That this isn't a passing whim?'

'Do you really want to know?' He was staring at her.

She looked at him then; the note in his voice demanded it. 'Yes.' But she wasn't sure if that was true.

'Because I didn't want to wake up beside the others for the rest of my life,' he said simply. There was a ringing silence but for the life of her she couldn't speak. 'What makes you so afraid of me, Rosie?' he asked very quietly.

Her heart was pounding. This shouldn't be happening now, not when his friend was so ill and he had to fly thousands of miles away. It wasn't fair to him. 'I...I didn't say I was frightened of you.'

'You don't have to.' He gave a short, mirthless laugh. 'But for the life of me I don't understand why. At first I thought it was something physical, especially because you haven't dated in so long, but we're fine that way, aren't we?'

It was a question and she answered it. 'I think so.'

'So I waited on that score, trying to show you in every way I could apart from the ultimate act that it would be fine, that I wouldn't hurt you, that you just had to relax and let yourself know me a little. But today—' He stopped abruptly, raking back his hair. 'You were with me every inch of the way.'

Her body was rigid, her head whirling.

'So what is it, Rosie?' he asked softly after a moment or two. 'Why don't you know how you feel? Why aren't you *letting* yourself know how you feel? It's all to do with your ex-husband. What the hell did he do to you?'

She bit her lip hard. She couldn't think clearly any more. She wished she could make some sense of how she felt but she couldn't pin down any logic. Her emotions had taken over her reason and paralysed her judgement. How could she make Kingsley understand where she was coming from when she didn't understand herself? But she had to try; after all he'd said she owed him that at least. She sucked in a gasp of air. 'Miles…Miles wasn't normal,' she said shakily.

There was silence. Then very gently he said, 'In what way wasn't he normal?'

'I…he…' Her voice faltered. 'I…need to explain from the beginning. I met him the first year at university and I thought he was wonderful. He was handsome, funny, everything a girl could wish for. I suppose he swept me off my feet. His family were well off and he was the only boy at university with a sports car, that sort of thing. This makes me sound so shallow,' she added shakily.

'No, just a normal eighteen-year-old away from everything she knows and in love for the first time,' he said softly.

She looked at him, stunned by his understanding.

'And?' He pressured her very gently to continue.

'And he wanted me. I…I hadn't slept with anyone before and I think he found that a challenge.'

Kingsley looked at the beautiful face with its silky veil of chestnut hair and his stomach contracted. Whatever this guy had done, hanging was too good for him.

'Anyway, we…we got married because I…' she forced herself to sit up straighter, aware she had been slumping '…because I didn't think it was right to go to bed otherwise. Up until then he'd been fun and charming but…he changed. Almost overnight. He—' she shut her eyes tightly, unable to look at him '—became violent. Over the slightest thing. But only when we were alone. Everyone else thought he was the perfect husband, and I was young and I thought it was all my fault so I tried to humour him. Looking back, I think that made him even more of a bully.'

'He hit you?' he said grimly, his guts writhing.

She nodded. 'Where it didn't show, mostly. He was clever like that. After the divorce an aunt of his contacted me—she was the only one of his family to do so—and she told me he had always been violent and cruel from a small boy, but that his parents had made excuses for him. He was unbalanced, she said, and took after his father's father who had ended his days in a psychiatric hospital.'

She was shaking, she couldn't help it, the shock of hearing herself talking to someone about Miles making her nauseous.

'What made you leave him in the end? I presume it *was* you who walked out?' he said carefully, aware from her white face and trembling body she was near the limit of her endurance.

'I found him in bed with someone else and when he hit me I hit back,' she whispered. 'It sent him crazy.' She could almost feel the clothes being torn off her back. 'He tried to—' She couldn't say it but he understood anyway. 'Our neighbour broke the door down and pulled him off me.' She shook her head blindly.

His arms came around her and he drew her against him but she couldn't relax against him, the shame and humiliation of that moment making her stiff and unyielding. If Robert hadn't helped her Miles would have raped her that night for sure, because she had been all but naked and helpless by then.

But Robert had proved himself to be a true friend. He hadn't spoken of what had occurred to anyone except her solicitor when she'd asked him to give a statement, and when Miles's parents had whisked him home and the rumours had started no one had known anything for sure. It had been the only thing that had enabled her to go on. To be able to hold her head up.

'Where is he now?' The words were full of a dark, vibrating energy. No one could have doubted why he was asking.

'He crashed his sports car, killing himself and the girl he was with some time ago,' she said shakily. 'The aunt wrote and told me.'

'Pity,' he growled. 'He got off lightly.'

'Maybe,' she said thickly, wondering why she didn't feel better for telling him. Wasn't that what all the books said, that you felt better when everything was out in the open?

'So he was the reason you decided to step out of the human race and become autonomous,' Kingsley said gently. 'I can understand that, truly, but don't let him still beat you down. This is different, *we're* different. You do see that, don't you?'

She moved out of his arms, away from him. Miles had used those very same words on the day he has asked her to be his wife. 'We're different to the rest of them, Lee,' he'd said, his handsome face smiling and his brown eyes dark and compelling. 'We're two halves of one whole and life is going to be perfect from now on. I promise you.'

Her hands were clenched together now, tension radiating from her. 'He talked like that,' she said almost to herself.

'Like what?'

She shook her head. 'It doesn't matter.'

'It does to me,' he said quietly, struggling for calmness. 'I don't like being compared to him, Rosie.'

'I didn't mean...' Her voice trailed away. Perhaps she did mean it. There were so many similarities between Miles and Kingsley, not just the good looks and wealth but their iron wills. She had never imagined in her worst nightmares that Miles was so twisted and cruel under his outward veneer; how could she be sure about Kingsley?

'I'm me, Rosie, not that creep you married.' He stated the obvious. 'And I love you.'

'When you told me about Maria you said love was just a pleasant concept, that it doesn't work in the real world,' she said flatly. 'Sooner or later doubt and mistrust happen, that's what you said.'

One half of him wanted to shake her for being this way, the other wanted to make all the hurt go away. His frustration and resentment at the way she was putting him in the same category as her former husband showed in his voice when he said, 'I was talking out of the back of my head, and men are allowed to change their minds occasionally—it isn't just a woman's prerogative. I want to be with you, Rosie. Always.'

'And if you change your mind again, what then?' she said tensely, her chin rising as she stared him straight in the face. Miles had said that she had trapped him, ruined his life. That she was nothing, a parasite, unloving and unlovable. She had fought back against allowing his mental abuse to penetrate her perception of herself for the last ten years; she wouldn't survive a second time. 'What if you're not cut out for togetherness? Would you think I'd trapped you; blame me for being around? Would you say you were tripping over me all the time, that you couldn't breathe—?'

'Did he do that?' Kingsley interrupted softly. 'Did he say all those things?'

She jerked her head back, self-protection written all

over her. 'It doesn't matter; what matters is that I don't want any of this. I'm sorry, but I don't. I was honest with you from the very beginning.'

'Yes, you were,' he agreed slowly. 'So, where do we go from here?'

She stared at him. She had never felt so wretched in all her life. 'There…there's nowhere *to* go.'

'I don't accept that,' he said impassively.

Her eyes widened. She had expected him to storm out and call it a day. 'Kingsley, I meant all I've said.'

'You think you mean it.' He was careful not to touch her; it would only complicate things further if he gave in to his desire to take her in his arms and kiss her until she agreed black was white. This was deeper than that. 'But I don't believe you do.'

He closed his eyes and settled back on the sofa again, stretching his long legs as he made himself comfortable.

There were minuscule particles of dust dancing in a patch of bright sunlight just above his head, and Rosalie's eyes were drawn to them as she rose to her feet. She stood uncertainly, an ache in her throat and a churning in her stomach, and found she didn't know what to say. She'd learnt enough about him over the past months, both from her own observations and from business colleagues—who talked avidly of his ruthless reputation—to know Kingsley was not renowned for an excess of patience. This wasn't like him. At least not as far as she knew. Which brought her right back to the point in question—how sure could she be about anything to do with him?

'Did someone mention coffee and brunch?' His tone was deep, the laconic request bringing her back to herself and she turned, walking into the kitchen on shaky legs.

She couldn't believe she had just told Kingsley, *Kingsley* of all people, about Miles and her marriage.

What was he thinking? She stood at the kitchen sink, gripping the porcelain so hard her knuckles shone white through her skin. Did he think she was pathetic and stupid? Was he disgusted, with her as well as Miles? Why, oh, why had she told him? She squeezed her eyes tight, trying to stop the hot tears from falling.

'It's all right.' She hadn't been aware of him following her, but now he enfolded her into his arms and she had no more strength left to resist. 'I know it took a lot of courage to tell me about him, but he's gone, Rosie,' he said over her head as he held her against the solid wall of his chest. 'You get men like him in every generation, emotional cripples who prey on the gentle and the good. They're inadequate and deep down they recognise it so they compensate with cruelness. I'm glad he's dead because it saves me hunting him out and dealing with him as he deserves. Telling me has brought it all back right now and exposed the wound, but wounds can heal, believe me, and it's better when they're cleaned out, however painful.'

It wasn't as simple as that. There was so much more to this than just her marriage, but she hadn't fully realised it till now. The violent death of her mother, her father's suicide, the years of wondering if she had contributed to her mother's death simply by being born, and then—when she'd thought Miles was the answer to all her hopes and dreams, when she'd found someone who would love her, *really* love her—the nightmare of her marriage and its cataclysmic end.

She was a mess. This wasn't about Kingsley, it was about *her*. She drew away, pushing back her hair from her face as she said quietly, 'I'll see to the food and I'll bring your coffee through when it's ready.'

He made no move to hold onto her and he didn't say

a word before he turned and left the kitchen, his eyes just
raking her white face for a moment.

They ate at the little pine table in a corner of her sitting
room and it brought back memories of the first time he
had been to the house, the evening he had brought her
home from the hospital. She should have made sure any
relationship between them had ended then. The thought
caused her throat to close up and she had to force herself
to eat, each mouthful threatening to choke her.

He glanced at his watch as they finished, his voice expressionless as he said, 'Are you coming to the airport
with me?'

She stared at him. 'Do you want me to?' she asked in
a small voice. 'After all that's been said?'

His voice held a touch of irritation as he said, 'Of
course I want you to. What sort of damn fool question is
that?'

She would have smiled if she had been able. His reply
was so very much Kingsley, and another strand of the
tensile net he'd thrown round her heart. A net she had to
break. She couldn't let herself love him or anyone else,
not again. She needed to be in control in every area of
her life and love took that away, giving a terrible power
to someone else.

She would go to the airport with him and she wouldn't
say anything more to rock the boat before he left, not in
view of the situation he had to deal with in Jamaica with
his friend. But this was the finish. It had to be. He just
didn't know it yet.

CHAPTER NINE

KINGSLEY took her hand in the taxi on the way to the airport and she let it lie there. They didn't talk but there was so much unsaid hanging between them that Rosalie felt the air were crackling. She was vitally aware of him at her side, his hard thigh touching hers and his big body seemingly relaxed. But he wasn't. She knew him well enough by now to know that he was playing a part, just as she was.

The airport was seething with people, and after Kingsley had checked in his luggage he took her arm and they made their way to one of the fast-food places. He ordered two coffees, which neither of them wanted, and once they were sitting on uncomfortable chairs at a table for two he took her hands in his. 'You're cold.' It was said with surprise.

She shrugged. She'd been chilled from the inside out since she'd decided what she had to do. 'My self air-conditioning has never been too good,' she said lightly.

Kingsley's eyes narrowed and he gave her a long look. 'I'm planning to come back at the end of the week,' he said quietly. 'Dinner on Friday night?'

'You might not be back,' she hedged quickly. 'Let's decide later.'

'No, let's decide now.'

Suddenly she felt they were discussing more than the dinner. She stared at him. He looked tough and strong, a man who would deal with any problem life presented and sort it out on his own terms. A man who wouldn't compromise, who would always want his own way because he would feel it was the best way. And yet he had been gentle and understanding with her, she had to admit that. And again this all came back to it being *her* who was the mixed-up kid, but she was a woman on her own—she had been for ten years—and she had managed just fine, hadn't she? She'd accepted she had to fight her own battles and stand on her own two feet and she had done it. Her life and what she did with it was down to her, and no one could rob her of that unless she gave over her independence, her self-respect, her autonomy.

True, the feelings of inadequacy that plagued her in the dark of the night were hard to deal with at times, especially since she had got to know Kingsley. She'd resolutely held back from giving way to the desire of imagining what it would be like to be in his arms, to have him holding her, loving her, banishing the demons with the strength of his presence. Dreams of that sort were all very well, but if they turned into nightmares…

'I wouldn't let you down, Rosie.' It was as though he had read her mind and she blinked at him. 'If I say Friday, I'll be here on Friday.' Again they both knew there was more to the conversation than the surface indicated. 'You are going to have to trust me sooner or later because I'm not going to go anywhere.'

'You're going to Jamaica,' she said, thinking, What a stupid thing to say at such a time.

'If you asked me to stay I would,' he said simply.

'What about your friend?'

'You come first.'

Her heart began to beat erratically. 'I wouldn't ask you to stay. You must go and see him; he needs you.'

'And you don't?'

She was silent. There was nothing she could say. Nothing at all.

He sighed irritably. 'I feel like I'm treading a minefield with you most of the time, do you know that? I never know when something I might say might be used against me, likened to the swine you married. You do that, don't you? Look for the same failings in me as you found in him?'

She was horrified and it showed, but she didn't deny it. How could she? It was true. And what man was going to put up with that in the months and years to come? Certainly not one like Kingsley who only had to click his fingers and have a hundred beauties lined up panting.

'If you think that...' Her voice trailed away.

'Why do I bother?' He finished the sentence for her. 'Why do you think I bother, Rosie? Why do you think I've been treading on eggshells the last few months? You've finally opened up about this sicko you married, but now the steel is inches thicker, isn't it?'

'What steel?'

'The stuff that coats the door to your heart,' he said, poetically for Kingsley.

There was a slight pause. 'I can't help how I feel,' she whispered, letting her hair fall in two wings at the side of her cheeks to hide her face from him and the tears she was struggling to keep behind her eyelids.

'Yes, you can,' he said, and his voice sounded oddly husky. 'Don't you think I went through hell when I realised I was falling in love with you? It's not just you who has the right to feel scared to death. After Maria I vowed I'd never let this happen again. Who needs it? A woman is a woman is a woman, and there were plenty out there who were only too willing to play the game the way I wanted it. Everything to gain and nothing to lose. Total safety. And then you came along.'

She didn't speak, she was crying, soundlessly, the tears slowly dripping down her cheeks, his honesty forcing her to admit what she had been trying to keep buried for weeks. She loved him. She had loved him for days, weeks, months, for ever. That was why the thought of giving herself to him terrified her so desperately. She loved him more than she had ever loved Miles, more than she would have thought herself capable of. Which meant his power over her was absolute. He mustn't know. He mustn't ever know.

He had stopped talking. He was breathing hard and she could feel he was looking at her although she didn't raise her head. After a moment a crisp white handkerchief was pushed into her hands. 'Don't cry.' His voice was gruff, painful. 'Damn it, the last thing I want to do is to make you cry. Drink your coffee.'

She wiped her face and drank the coffee, which was lukewarm and tasted foul, and then she raised her eyes, knowing his would be waiting for her. 'It would never work, Kingsley, you and I,' she said shakily. 'I'd spoil anything you're feeling for me right now because I can't be what you want me to be. When Miles did what he did—' she stopped, wondering how to explain the unexplainable '—something died,' she finished slowly. 'Something I can't get back.'

'I don't believe that,' he said with quiet emphasis. 'I love you, damn it, and I want to marry you and have children and grow old with you. I'm not Miles, I'm not anyone but myself and I've allowed you to see what that is, who I am. That has to count for something on this scorecard you keep in your head.'

She tore her gaze from his, wondering why she had

been so foolish as to come here with him. But she knew the answer to that. She'd wanted to be with him, this one last time. Every minute, every second was precious, and they were spending it arguing. She spoke the thought out loud. 'I don't want to fight, there's not much time.'

'I've never ducked an issue in my life and I'm blowed if I'll start with the most important one that's ever come my way,' he said grimly. 'I'll take a later plane if necessary.'

She shrank inwardly. She couldn't cope with much more of this. It was tearing her apart. 'Don't be silly,' she whispered brokenly. 'Your friend is waiting for you.'

'You don't get it, do you?' His voice was suddenly very quiet. 'You really don't get it. You don't have the faintest idea what you mean to me.'

'*I don't want to.*' It was wrenched out of her. 'This is hard enough as it is. Can't you accept I mean what I say and leave me alone? This is for the best and you'll see it one day.'

'The hell I will.' His mouth came down on hers and he kissed her hard, oblivious to anyone else.

'No.' She jerked her head away, panic-stricken. She couldn't weaken now and she always did when he touched her. This had to be the end, now, right here. He was away for a few days and it would give him time to reflect, to see she was right. They had no future. She loved him too much for there to be a possibility of a future but she couldn't say that, he wouldn't understand. But she mustn't weaken. He was too formidable an opponent, too intelligent and intuitive for her to show a chink in the steel he'd spoken of. 'I don't want this. I don't want you.'

He looked her straight in the eyes, his gaze so piercingly blue it was painful to hold. 'You don't mean that.'

'I do.' She nodded, her head wagging as though it were

on strings. 'I do mean it. And you've got to go. You'll miss your plane.'

He said something very rude about the plane, which made a passing customer gasp in shock and hurry to the other end of the seating area.

'I can't cope with you in my life, Kingsley. Is that plain enough?' she said desperately. 'I want it to be like it used to be before I met you. Mike or one of the others can take over the job from now on.'

'I don't want Mike or one of the others. The contract says you.'

'Then I'll resign and you can sue me if you want.' She glared at him, fear and defiance in her face.

He was silent for what seemed like a long, long time, his face full of a bewildered anger that cut her in two. 'You needn't resign your job,' he said at last. 'Not because of me. Put Mike on my project if you like, or one of the others. I really don't care.'

He stood up slowly, his face grey under his tan. 'Goodbye, Rosie.'

'Goodbye.'

She was conscious of a screaming toddler to the left of her who had just flung orange juice all over its mother, and two teenagers in the corner who were giggling at a magazine they had propped between them.

Something as momentous as their breaking up shouldn't happen in such mundane surroundings surely? she thought dazedly.

He looked at her one last time but he didn't speak again, merely giving her a curt nod and turning away, walking with calm, measured steps out of the restaurant and out of her life. And she let him go.

*   *   *

'You've done *what*?'

Rosalie winced at the pitch of Beth's voice. 'I've split with Kingsley,' she repeated flatly. 'It's over.'

It was Sunday afternoon and she was sitting in Beth's garden engulfed in the perfume of roses, honeysuckle and a hundred and one other scents from the profuse blooms adorning every nook and cranny, not to mention the flowerbeds. It was hot, it was very hot and a storm was imminent, but in spite of the weather Beth had cooked a big Sunday roast with all the trimmings, which Rosalie had ploughed through as best she could, considering every mouthful felt as though it would choke her. She hadn't slept a wink all night and had been prowling the flat at four in the morning crying her eyes out.

'But he adored you, anyone could see that,' Beth said agitatedly. 'Don't tell me another woman hooked him? I don't believe it.'

'You don't have to, it didn't happen like that,' Rosalie said carefully. 'We just felt it wasn't right, that's all.'

'We?' Beth looked at Rosalie's puffy eyes. 'The rotten, two-timing rat.'

'Beth, I promise you, Kingsley didn't do anything wrong,' Rosalie protested. 'There's no other woman, believe me.' Not yet anyway. 'It was just getting a bit…serious, that's all.'

'Oh, Lee.' Beth's voice dropped in horror. 'You didn't.'

'Didn't what?' Rosalie said uncomfortably.

'Freeze him out? Not Kingsley. Not the most gorgeous man you're ever likely to meet.' There was a slight pause, and then Beth said, 'You did, didn't you? And you're regretting it already.'

For the first time Rosalie could understand why Beth's children had been eager to escape the nest as soon as they could. There was something terribly annoying about someone who was always right.

'I'm not regretting it, not really,' she said flatly. 'It's for the best in the long run. He wanted more than I could give.'

'Sex without any commitment? Typical man. Is that it?'

'Not exactly.'

'You to move in with him? Bad mistake. You lose your independence and he keeps his. I can see—'

'*Beth.*' She was trying very hard to be patient. 'He wanted to—' She stopped. She didn't know how to put this. 'He was talking marriage,' she said at last.

'No…' It was a long drawn-out gasp. 'And you said no? Lee, are you mad?'

Perhaps it hadn't been such a good idea to come here today, but she couldn't have faced any of her friends feeling the way she did, and staying brooding in the flat just hadn't been an option.

'Probably.' She didn't smile. 'Very probably. He thinks I am, anyway. It wasn't an…amicable parting.' Her voice had quivered on the last words.

'Oh, baby.' Beth did what she did best and turned mother earth, springing up and kneeling down beside Rosalie's chair and hugging her tight.

It started an avalanche of tears that shocked them both and caused George, who had just wandered out from his study for a few moments, to beat a hasty retreat back indoors.

Over several glasses of Beth's iced lemonade liberally laced with lime and crushed raspberries, Rosalie told Beth the whole story throughout the sticky afternoon, discussing her fears and doubts for the second time in as many days but this time with someone who had no axe to grind. They were no nearer a solution when the heat of the day had gone and evening shadows spangled the slanting sunlight, and Rosalie couldn't honestly say she felt better for discussing the whole sorry mess, but, nevertheless, she was glad she had come to see her aunt. It had been hard to talk about Miles and exactly what had happened in their marriage, but strangely not as hard as she'd expected, perhaps because telling Kingsley had broken some mental barrier that had been in place before.

'I always loathed him, but then you know that,' Beth said of Miles. 'In all the time you were with him we hardly saw anything of you. It was all *his* friends, *his* interests, wasn't it?'

'I guess so.' Rosalie nodded. In that way Miles had been like her father, although her father's motive had sprung from a misguided, warped jealousy born of love, and Miles's had been pure selfishness. 'I didn't notice it at first as all our friends were mutual.'

'Kingsley isn't like him, Lee. You do know that, don't you?' Beth said earnestly as they made their goodbyes in the cool of the evening. 'He wouldn't use force or be violent. I know it.'

She nodded. 'I know it too, it's not that. But...' She shook her head slowly. 'I think I'm too scared by marriage to ever want to take a chance again, and then other times over the last twenty-four hours I'm almost picking up the phone to try and contact him and tell him I need him. How's that for inconsistency?'

'Perhaps if you said you'd live with him, without the marriage bit?' suggested Beth, the most staunch advocator of marriage in the whole of London, who drove her children mad by insisting anything else was living in sin.

Rosalie gave her aunt a hug. 'Beth, I'm really going to miss you,' she said, meaning it. 'But it's not even the marriage thing, although that is a sign of huge commitment. It's more...letting him know how much I love him, you know? Miles would always belittle me to puff himself

up and I know Kingsley wouldn't do that, but when someone is sure of your love they can change...' Her voice
trailed away as she gazed at her aunt. 'Oh, I don't know
how to put it,' she said flatly. 'I just know it scares me
to death.'

Beth looked at her for a long moment. 'And how much
does *not* being with him scare you?' she said softly. 'And
don't answer now,' she added as Rosalie opened her
mouth. 'Think about it. All right?'

Rosalie did think about it. She thought about it all through
the next few nights when she tossed and turned until dawn
in the sticky heat, the anticipated storm and change in the
weather yet to make an appearance.

She woke very early on the Friday morning when
Kingsley was due back, even though she hadn't managed
to fall to sleep until way after two.

She had made the worst mistake of her life. Even mar-
rying Miles paled into insignificance beside sending
Kingsley away. Suddenly her mind was crystal clear for
the first time since she had met him and she knew exactly
what she wanted.

Miles was gone—in every sense of the word. Gone
from her mind, her heart, her life and this world, so what
was she doing letting him ruin her life for the second
time? Beth was right, the possibility of *not* being with
Kingsley scared her a hundred times more than accepting
him fully into her life.

Kingsley was nothing like Miles, not in character and
he had shown her that. His honesty, his straightness, his
ability to face issues head-on—Miles had had none of
those qualities. Miles had been a pile of dead men's bones
beneath the outward façade of handsomeness and debo-
nair conviviality, nothing about the person he had pre-

tended to be before they'd married had been real. And she had allowed a man like that to convince her that love meant constriction and fear.

She sat up in bed, turning on the bedside lamp and staring into the dimly lit room. What a fool she'd been, what a blind, stupid fool. Kingsley had bared his heart to her, given everything he knew how to give and she hadn't even listened to him, not really. What had she done?

Her stomach twisted and she climbed out of bed, padding along to the kitchen and making herself a strong cup of coffee.

Why hadn't she found the courage to tell him she loved him? she asked herself helplessly. He hadn't phoned or contacted her since he'd gone and she didn't blame him. He'd clearly washed his hands of her. But how could she live in a world in which Kingsley was living, and not be with him? To know he was free to meet someone else, to marry someone else, to have babies with someone else.

She groaned, laying her head on the cool surface of the breakfast bar for a moment. She wanted to be with him more than anything in the world but she'd been too hung up by the terrors of the past to recognise it. When he'd left she'd thought a few days' separation would make him see that she was right and that they had no future together. What if that was exactly what he *did* think? How ironic when she'd done a full hundred-and-eighty-degree turn, if he'd done the same.

She drank the coffee scalding hot, and it was as she finished the last mouthful that she thought, What am I doing? What *am* I doing? If he loved her, if he *really* loved her it would be with warts, pimples and all. That was the sort of guy he was. So…did she believe he really loved her? She felt a surge of joy such as she hadn't felt since she'd been very young rise up. Yes, she did. She did. So it was logical to believe he hadn't changed his mind. Her fears and emotions might lead her down one path but she had to stand on logic and trust. She couldn't keep doubting him or herself, not if this relationship was going to have any future. And she wanted a future with Kingsley, oh, so much.

She found herself pacing the small kitchen and stopped abruptly, realising she was so tense her hands were clenched tight.

A bath. And then a call to the airport to see what time his flight arrived. She'd meet him. Whatever time he landed she'd be there waiting for him. She glanced at the kitchen clock. In fact she'd call the airport first, just in case it was an early arrival.

They were very sorry, the anonymous voice at the airport said politely, but there were no flights arriving from Jamaica today. Hadn't she heard about the cyclone?

No, she hadn't, Rosalie said tightly.

Cyclone Kimberley was heading straight for the coast and unfortunately holding course despite all predictions it would swing away; consequently all flights were cancelled for the foreseeable future. If she would like to ring tomorrow they might have news then.

She put the telephone down very carefully, her hands shaking. And then picked it up immediately to phone Kingsley's secretary in England for details of where he was staying, before she remembered it wasn't yet five o'clock.

The next four hours were the longest of her life.

She had a bath and washed her hair, cleaned the kitchen from top to bottom, including washing the inside of the cupboards and rearranging everything, after which she rearranged it all back again. Her mind was plaguing her with vivid pictures. Kingsley buried under a pile of debris.

Kingsley trapped and injured or worse. And all the time thinking she didn't love him, that she didn't want him. She couldn't bear it. She just couldn't bear it.

She phoned Jenny at home at eight o'clock, explaining she had a few things she needed to sort out and that she wouldn't be in the office until much later, if at all. Apart from a little juggling with a couple of afternoon appointments there was nothing too vital to sort out.

At nine she spoke to Kingsley's secretary in the office at Oxford. 'Oh, hello, Miss Milburn,' the girl said politely. 'Mr Ward's number in Jamaica? Sure, I have it here. Just a minute.' There was the sound of rustling paper, and then the disembodied voice said quietly, 'Awful about his friend, isn't it? And not been long married too. And now there's all this panic about the cyclone.'

Rosalie's heart was lurching. 'His friend hasn't...?'

'Oh, no, he hasn't died, but it looks like he's paralysed, although they can't move him yet to a hospital in the States.'

'Right.' She took down the number, gave her thanks and put the receiver down, aware her hands were shaking so badly the numbers were barely recognisable.

It was around three in the morning in Jamaica—should she wait a while or phone now? Selfishly, she admitted, she was going to phone now. She needed to talk to him, to tell him how she felt, and she might not be able to get through anyway if the cyclone had hit. Her stomach went over at the thought.

The hotel receptionist sounded weary—no doubt she had been taking calls from anxious relatives and friends for most of the night—but she put Rosalie through to Kingsley's room without any argument, after indicating Mr Ward might have already joined a number of other guests who were preparing to shelter in the basement.

The phone was picked up immediately. 'Hello?'

'Kingsley, is that you?' Stupid opening line considering it was hardly likely to be anyone else. 'It's Rosalie.'

'Rosie?'

She was fighting back the tears that had sprung up with relief at hearing his voice and couldn't continue for a minute, and as the line cracked and popped his voice came again, louder, saying. 'Rosie? Are you there?'

'I'm so sorry.' Her bottom lip was trembling so much it was hard to speak. 'Can you ever forgive me?'

'Rosie, I can't hear you—the storm—you'll have to shout.'

'Can you ever forgive me?' she bellowed down the line, the urgency of it all providing the shot of adrenalin she needed to pull herself together. 'I've been so stupid.'

'You're not stupid—' The line faded and then crackled, and his voice came back again, saying, '…very brave, don't you know that?'

'I can't hear you!'

'I said you are the gutsiest woman I know and very brave. Look, it's getting worse—' there were a few more frustrating moments when the line shuddered and died, and then '—get back.'

'What? Oh, Kingsley, I can't hear you and I want to say I'm sorry and that I love you and that you must be careful.' But he was saying something too and she was almost sure he couldn't hear her.

'Kingsley, if you need to go and shelter, do it. I love you. Let me know you're all right when you can.' But the line had gone dead. She put down the receiver and burst into tears. He was in danger, and she wasn't sure if he knew she loved him or had heard anything she'd said.

She spent the rest of the day glued to the TV and radio reports, getting more and more worked up as they confirmed that Cyclone Kimberley was a biggie and was taking no prisoners. Rosalie drank numerous cups of coffee but couldn't eat a thing, and when Beth called in the evening, having heard the news on the TV, which had mentioned all power lines were down along with pretty severe destruction in places, she was all but climbing the walls.

'I'm coming over,' Beth said, at the sound of Rosalie's agitated voice.

'No, it's all right, really.'

'I'm coming. George is away at some conference or other and won't get back till tomorrow, and at least it won't seem so bad if there's two of us worrying together. Have you eaten?' she added in true mother-hen fashion.

'I don't want anything.'

'See you in a little while.'

Before she knew it Beth was on the doorstep, her arms full of tubs and boxes from an Indian take-away, along with a couple of bottles of wine.

'I'm…not hungry.' Rosalie was determined she wasn't going to cry again. She hadn't cried in years before she'd met Kingsley, but since he'd come into her life it seemed as if she'd done little else.

Beth ignored her, bustling about the kitchen heating food in the microwave and opening a bottle of very good red wine, saying as she did so, 'Listen to me, Lee. There have been worse cyclones than this one, much worse, and Jamaica and other such places are geared up for them. They're a yearly hazard, for goodness' sake, like…like snowstorms here.'

Rosalie's expression indicated what she thought of such a pathetic comparison.

'Kingsley's going to be absolutely fine, I know it, and you won't do him or yourself any good if you make yourself ill, now then. You are going to eat and drink, and wait for him to call you. Power lines always go down with these sorts of things, along with roofs being blown away and the odd boat or two being sunk, but that doesn't mean anyone gets hurt. I told you, they know what to do.'

Beth handed Rosalie a large glass of red wine. 'Drink some, *now*,' she commanded in the same voice she used to her offspring when it was a case of 'she who must be obeyed'.

Rosalie drank. The rich and full-bodied wine with the aroma of raspberries, damsons and spices left a warm glow and steadied the trembling in her stomach.

'Now go and set the table for two,' Beth said briskly, handing her the bottle and another glass. 'We're eating first and then you can tell me all about it.'

Amazingly Rosalie found she managed a good assault on her heaped plate before finally admitting defeat when it was half empty, another glass of wine helping enormously in forcing the food down.

After she had filled Beth in on her decision and the position to date, the two women sat sipping wine and talking until far into the night. Eventually, at gone two, Beth persuaded her to go to bed, insisting she would sit and doze in a chair by the phone.

'You look awful,' Beth said with her usual honesty. 'Get some sleep or you'll be meeting him with bags under your eyes big enough to shop with.'

Rosalie climbed into bed complaining that this was a wasted exercise and she wouldn't sleep a wink, and it was much more sensible for Beth to have her bed. However, she was asleep as soon as her head touched the pillow, the lack of rest over the last few days and the relaxing effect of the wine causing a deep, dreamless slumber.

She only slept for four hours, her subconscious then

kicking in and reminding her she ought to be awake and worrying, but she felt better for it as she tottered into the sitting room where Beth was snoring softly in her chair by the phone.

Beth went home after lunch, Rosalie having promised her aunt she would phone her as soon as she heard anything, and it seemed as though no sooner had the other woman left than the telephone rang.

'Rosie?'

It was Kingsley. She felt her heart give an almighty jump and then start thumping away like a sledgehammer. 'Kingsley.' She knew her voice sounded choked but she couldn't help it. 'Kingsley, I love you,' she said desperately, terrified they would lose the connection again. 'I was wrong about everything and I want us to be together. Can you hear me?'

'I can hear you, sweetheart.'

Sweetheart. He'd called her sweetheart. The tears were dripping down her face again but she didn't care. She'd cry every day all day if it meant he called her sweetheart.

'Listen, I've found a guy with a satellite mobile, there's still a virtual shut-down here, but he needs to make some urgent business calls so I need to talk fast.'

'Are you all right? You're not injured?'

'Filthy dirty, hungry, thirsty, but no, not injured. There's massive structural damage, especially in the shanty towns, and a number of us are helping out.'

'Oh, be careful. Don't take any chances.' She immediately had visions of buildings falling down the moment he went near them.

'I'm glad you phoned last night.' His voice was soft now, deep, and she shivered.

'So am I.'

'I love you.'

'I love you too.' She suddenly remembered she hadn't asked about his friend. 'How's Alex?' she said quickly.

'Not good.' Suddenly she could hear the exhaustion in his voice. 'I really needed that phone call from you. Fortunately the cyclone missed the hospital he's in so that's something.'

'Kingsley, you do forgive me?'

'Always, sweetheart.'

She gulped, giving an involuntary sniff. 'When do you think you'll be able to leave the island?'

'We're waiting to hear. Look, I have to go. See you soon.'

No, no, not yet. She wanted to protest, feeling something would go wrong, something would happen before she saw him again and really made everything all right. Instead she said, 'Take care.'

'I will. Goodbye, Rosie.'

'Goodbye.'

There was so much she'd wanted to say. As soon as she put the receiver down she went over their conversation in her mind. She needed to make him understand what had held her back from making a commitment, why she loved him so much, how special he was, just everything.

She sat for a few minutes collecting her thoughts and reliving the moment he'd called her sweetheart, and then telephoned Beth, who was ecstatic for her. Dear, dear Beth.

She walked into the bedroom and, fully dressed as she was, climbed into bed after kicking off her shoes and slept for several hours.

She awoke to the telephone ringing again and virtually fell out of bed, hearing Beth's voice with a disappointment that made her bite her lip.

'Sorry, Lee, did you think it was him?' Beth said cheerfully. 'It's just that I wondered if you've got the TV on? They're doing a bit on the news about the cyclone in a minute or two and I thought you might be interested.'

Not unless they could arrange a one-to-one with Kingsley for her. 'Thanks.' She put as much enthusiasm in her voice as she could. 'I'll switch it on now.'

Ten minutes later she sat as though turned to stone, the bottom having dropped out of her world.

CHAPTER TEN

'LEE, I'm sure there's some sort of reasonable explanation. Don't make up your mind about anything until you've heard what he has to say.'

Rosalie listened to Beth who had phoned moments after the news item had ended, politely agreeing and saying she was perfectly all right about it all, before putting down the phone.

She sat in the quiet of her sitting room for a long time, trying to make sense of it all. In the end, she knew she couldn't.

The news crew had veered towards the humanitarian aspect of the natural disaster, emphasising it was the poorest who had been affected most by the cyclone but that on such desperate occasions man's humanity to man could spring into action. Holiday-makers and visitors from abroad in the area had all pulled together with the rescue services to help those injured or trapped under the debris of their houses in the shanty towns, it had proclaimed, showing pictures of the good Samaritans in action. 'Courage and hope mingling with helplessness and despair' type of reporting.

Her heart had nearly leapt out of her chest when she had seen Kingsley. Her breath caught at the memory. Her body felt strange, all tight and hurting, as though she had been pummelled and kicked about by something.

He had been in the background actually involved in digging an elderly man out from under the tin shack that had been his home until a tree had demolished it. A miraculous escape, the man they'd been interviewing had said. Part of the roof had fallen in such a way that the man had been cushioned in a small chamber and was virtually unhurt.

Her eyes had been fixed on the tall dark figure in the background and she had barely noticed anyone else—until Kingsley had been joined by a certain familiar and voluptuous brunette, that was. And Little Miss Canary hadn't been at all shy about kissing him full on the lips as she'd flung herself into his arms.

The broadcast had shifted at this point to the story of a little girl, who had managed to save the family's goat by untying the animal from where it had been tethered in the nick of time and bringing it into their house, which had survived the tropical storm, but the images of Kingsley with the woman who was his friend's sister were burnt onto the screen of Rosalie's mind.

She exhaled sharply. Even Beth had been forced to admit that the kiss hadn't been a sisterly one, and as Kingsley's arms had gone round the girl she had pressed herself into him with all the finesse of a bitch on heat.

She could understand Alex's sister coming to see her brother after the accident, of course she could, and Kingsley had known her for years, but that kiss…

What was she going to do? Reality hit, and with it a gut-wrenching pain. Her body ached as it did when she had the flu but this wasn't a virus, unless you could call love a virus? Maybe you could at that, she reflected silently. She swallowed hard.

What had she said to herself only twenty-four hours ago when she had decided that she was going to plunge head first into this relationship? Her fears and emotions might lead her down a certain path, but she had to stand on logic and trust. Logic and trust were all very well but when millions of people had seen the man she loved embrace another woman…

Logic—Miss Canary had embraced him. Trust—maybe he could give her an explanation as to why Alex's sister thought she had the right to give him a body massage but without using her hands? And maybe pigs could fly. Helplessness at her ability to contact Kingsley right at this second and ask him what the hell he thought he was playing at gripped her.

Could she envisage a future with a man she couldn't trust? Would Kingsley want a future with a woman he felt didn't trust him?

Rosalie stood up, walking out of the sitting room and into the bathroom, where she washed her tear-stained face before straightening and looking at herself in the small round mirror set over the basin. Tragic, tear-swept eyes stared back at her from a face even her nearest and dearest would have to admit was blotchy.

She'd had enough of crying. The thought sent something hot and deliberate coursing through her blood, and she took a deep breath, speaking it loud. 'I am sick and tired of crying.' The eyes applauded her stand. She wasn't going to do it any more. Kingsley would contact her soon. Her throat tightened. And she wasn't going to play any games or pretend she was feeling anything else than what she was feeling. She would ask him about the Canary calmly and composedly, but only when she saw him face to face. That way she would know if he was lying.

Her whole instinct was to run at the moment. Run from any commitment, run from confrontation, run from Kingsley, from love. But she was a grown woman now, not a scared, confused little child who had just lost the two people she cared about most in the world, or a broken young teenager whose love had been trampled into the ground in the cruellest way imaginable.

She had to face this head-on. Not hysterically, admittedly, but neither was she going to brush what she'd seen aside and pretend it wasn't real. She'd done that with Miles, she realised suddenly. Ignored the tell-tale signs of his affairs because she hadn't been able to bear to think he would do that to her. But he had. And because *he* was weak and flawed, not because she hadn't been enough for him. As Kingsley had said, Miles had been an emotional cripple, inadequate and cruel. *Kingsley.* Oh, Kingsley, Kingsley. Please come through for me. Please give me an answer that I can believe because it's true.

He phoned her the next day. 'I'm coming home, Rosie.' She liked the way he said home, and then warned herself not to get too starry-eyed so she couldn't see clearly when she asked him about Tweety Pie. 'I land at Heathrow at seven on Monday evening.'

'I'll meet you,' she offered carefully.

'I was hoping you'd say that.'

He was smiling, she knew he was smiling, and for a moment she felt anger that he was all hunky-dory and smiling, and she felt wretched. She took a deep breath. 'How are the cleaning-up operations going out there?'

'Not too bad. It's tough when you see the poverty and some of the locals have lost everything, but it's incredible how they pull together. Family is strong out here, that's the thing.'

'And Alex?' she asked even more carefully.

'The doctor his father brought out with him from the States says he can safely be moved at the end of next week, but he's already seeing signs he feels are hopeful.

How hopeful will depend on the tests they run in the hospital back home. Rosie—'

'His father?' She interrupted his voice, which had gone into silky soft mode when he'd said her name. She couldn't handle how it made her feel right now and she needed to be strong. 'It's not just his wife who's out there with you, then?' she asked, thinking, *As if I didn't know*.

'No, they're all here.'

Aren't they just? 'Right.' Full marks for the cheerfulness, Rosalie.

'What's wrong?' he asked softly.

Or perhaps not full marks, then. 'Wrong?' Everything. 'Nothing,' she lied firmly.

'I don't believe you but I have to go. Take care, sweetheart. I'll see you tomorrow. I love you.'

'I love you.' At least she could say that and mean it. But the people who were supposed to love you the best always ended up hurting you. She closed her eyes for some time after she'd replaced the receiver. Was Kingsley going to hurt her? She had already hurt him when she had sent him away.

It was a different variation on what she'd been thinking since she had decided she wanted to be with him, and her brow wrinkled. He had conquered his demons for her but she had unwittingly given him a few more when she had refused him before he'd left for Jamaica. And now she might hurt him again when she asked him about Alex's sister. But he was a man, not a child. She had pussyfooted about with Miles, scared of hurting him or making him angry. If Kingsley was the one for her he would meet her halfway. He might not like what she asked but he could handle it. That was the sort of man he was. The ache inside her deepened.

She wanted to believe in a love that would last for ever.

She couldn't believe how much she wanted to. But that wasn't wrong or weak, was it? She had only stopped wishing for it when the hurt of being disappointed had been too much to bear, but since Kingsley she had dared to hope again.

Would she have the courage to ask him about Alex's sister when he was standing in front of her, and she could see what she might lose? She hoped so. She didn't want to be disappointed in herself just when she was beginning to like what she saw in the mirror for the first time since she had been five years old.

She got to the airport early, not because she had planned to but because she couldn't help herself.

She had agonised over what to wear since she'd left work at the unheard-of time of four o'clock in the afternoon, and the entire contents of her wardrobe were now strewn over her bed at the flat. Ridiculous. She wrinkled her nose at herself and then moved her head to catch her reflection in the shiny surface of a snack dispensing machine.

She had gone from sophisticated to smart casual to casual and then back to sophisticated again about ten times in the last three hours, but eventually she'd let the weather decide for her. Lightning was flashing in weird jagged streaks across the rooftops and thunder was rolling ominously, but as yet there was no rain, just a stifling heat that was oppressive. She had chosen a light, spaghetti-strap silk crêpe dress in white, which fell to just above her ankles and which was wonderfully cool, dressing it down with slip-on cork sandals. Simple, chic and with just the right touch of 'I haven't dressed like this especially for you, I always look this good'.

The plane was on time and her thudding heart belied

the outward picture of cucumber-cool, composed feminin-
ity that had more than one pair of interested male eyes
turning Rosalie's way. But she didn't notice any of them.
All her senses were tied up with the watching for
Kingsley.

And then she saw him. Tall, confident and incredibly
handsome. She thought, I've bared my soul to this man,
told him things I'd never planned to tell anyone. How had
it all happened? And then he saw her, raising his hand as
his face broke into the smile that never ceased to make
her heart jump.

'Hi.' He reached her, dropping his case and taking her
in his arms. He bent down, pressing his mouth against
hers and his lips were warm and firm, the familiar delicious smell of him teasing her nostrils and the hard body
sending tingles down her spine. The kiss only lasted moments but she was trembling when he let her go, brushing
a wisp of hair from her forehead with the tip of one finger
as he said, 'You look beautiful, incredible.'

'Incredible's overdoing it a bit,' she managed fairly
lightly, 'but I'll take beautiful.'

''My pleasure.' He grinned at her and her senses went
into hyperdrive as his hands cupped her face as though
he couldn't bear not to touch her. 'I've dreamt of you
every night,' he said softly, 'but there's nothing like the
real thing.'

Kingsley, oh, Kingsley. I didn't want to fall in love
with you, that hadn't been the plan, but how do you stop
an unstoppable force?

She glanced at the sea of people, her voice small as she
said, 'Let's go, shall we?'

He looked at her, a searching look, but said nothing,
simply reaching for his case and then tucking her arm in

his as though it should be there. And she wanted it to be. So much.

Once outside she became aware that the first fat rain-drops were falling from a sky that looked like something from a science fiction film. 'The storm's breaking at last,' she said quietly. How strange. It had hung on for days and it had to be the minute they'd met again that the elements unleashed their fury.

Kingsley had just hailed a taxi when the heavens let loose with a sheet of water that had her soaked before she could scramble in. Once in the taxi she realised that the dress that had been so chic and elegant moments before was now completely see-through, hugging her body in a way that would win first prize in any wet T-shirt com-petition.

'Hell!' Kingsley raked back his dripping hair, the thin black shirt and trousers he was wearing soaked through but still decent. 'What is it about me that brings storm and tempest?'

It was said jokingly but something in her face caught his attention, and as the taxi driver began to move gin-gerly away, windscreen wipers at Olympic speed, he reached for her again, drawing her into him as he said, 'Okay, what is it? And don't say nothing,' and now there was no amusement in the deep voice. 'This was supposed to be the grand reunion, not a tragedy.'

She shivered, and not just because she was wet through. He had given her flat as their destination, and she had been hoping to wait until they were inside before saying anything. She felt the warmth of his body begin to warm her and she sucked in a breath. She might ruin everything here. She wanted to touch him and hold him, talk with him, love him. But she had to know. She didn't know how to start. 'Did you really dream of me?' she asked a little breathlessly.

'Sure.' He moved his head, looking down at her with eyes as blue and clear as sapphires. 'But if I'd seen you in this dress before it would definitely have featured.'

'I didn't realise it went see-through in the rain.'

'I'm not complaining. It's all the welcome homes I've ever had rolled into one.' He tilted her chin, kissing her nose and then her eyelids before taking her mouth in a kiss that immediately made her want more. And then he said, 'So? Spill.'

No accusations. You're asking the question, that's all. 'I saw you on the news,' she blurted out, not at all as she'd meant to start.

'What?' Whatever he'd been expecting, it was clear it wasn't this.

'On the news,' she repeated. 'They were interviewing someone about the cyclone and you were in the background, helping to rescue an old man?' She was looking at him very carefully.

'Well, I'll be blowed.' He grinned at her. 'I'd have sent you a kiss if I'd known.'

She stiffened; she couldn't help it. 'Actually you were already busy in that realm.' She raised her eyebrows questioningly but she had lost him, she could see it in his puzzled face.

'What realm?' he said easily.

'The kissing realm,' she said tightly. What else?

'Rosie, forgive me, but I haven't the faintest idea what you're talking about.'

'You don't remember?' Was that a good sign or a bad sign?

He frowned, his voice holding a thread of impatience.

'We could go on all night like this, so why don't you say what's on your mind and be done with it?'

'You and the canary.' Damn, she hadn't meant that to slip out. Blushing furiously, she qualified, 'You and Alex's sister.'

'Alex's...?' His brow cleared. 'You mean Trixie was in the shot? Is that what you're getting at?'

Trixie? Oh, her name wasn't really Trixie, was it? Her grandmother had had an incontinent poodle called Trixie. 'Not just in the shot,' she said evenly. 'You were kissing.'

He stared at her, his eyes narrowing, and she stared back, not at all sure how he was going to react. She tried to read his expression but she couldn't. She didn't know what he was thinking or feeling. So much for being able to read his face when she challenged him about it, she thought miserably.

'Where does the canary come in?' he asked after a long moment or two, when the only sound was the violent swishing of water from the windscreen wipers and the drumming of rain on the taxi's roof.

Rosalie shifted uncomfortably, and then became aware that the movement emphasised the taut peaks of her nipples through her damp clothes. Kingsley was aware of it too if the look on his face was anything to go by.

He eventually managed to tear his eyes away, saying again, 'The canary? I'm sorry but I don't follow. Why a canary?'

'I... You...weren't supposed to hear that. It slipped out.' Her face felt as though it were going to catch fire.

Dark eyebrows rose. He was demanding an answer.

'I saw her on the pictures of Alex's wedding, when you were the best man and she was the chief bridesmaid. She...she was dressed in yellow.'

He continued to study her hot face for a second more

and then he began to shake with laughter, much to Rosalie's chagrin.

'And she was draped all over you then,' she continued, and sharply now. 'And you looked as though you were enjoying it.'

'Now hold on a minute.' Still grinning, he shook his head. 'Trixie is the baby sister I never had. I indulge her, spoil her, tease her, but the thought of anything along the lines you're suggesting is ridiculous. Damn it, she's a baby.'

'A baby?' Rosalie had promised herself she wouldn't get mad but he was the limit. 'A baby with a thirty-eight, twenty-four, thirty-six shape is no baby, Kingsley, and you might not have noticed but the "baby" has got the hots for you,' she finished somewhat crudely.

'Rosie, she's twenty years old.'

'So? How many men do you know that have girlfriends who are ten, twenty, thirty years younger than them? It isn't exactly unheard of,' she said scathingly.

'You're jealous.' He was clearly delighted and she could have killed him. Is this what she'd suffered the torments of the damned for? She took back all the nice thoughts she'd had.

'Not at all.' She drew herself up and away from him, as regally as the transparent dress would allow. 'I just think it's pretty disgusting to carry on the way she does in public, that's all.'

'You are, aren't you?' It was faintly wondering and actually doused her anger more effectively than anything else could have done. 'You're jealous of a silly little girl who hasn't a grain of sense in her head and is a damn sight more irritating than anything else. The child's a pest, Rosie. She always has been. She drives me mad half the time, if you want to know, but, like I said, she's the kid sister and so I don't mind.'

She stared at him, barely hearing him past the 'silly little girl' bit. He meant it, she thought in amazement. He actually thought that gorgeous young thing was a pest. She still said, 'You were kissing,' in a faintly stubborn voice, unable to give in completely. 'And she definitely doesn't want you for a brother.'

'She kissed me, if I remember, and, as she'd come with the news that the doctors were more hopeful about Alex for the first time since he was injured, I might have held her for a moment. And she's at an age where she's finding her wings—she flirts with any and every man. It doesn't mean a thing.'

She stared at him, all eyes, and his voice changed, becoming softer as he murmured, 'Come here, my love.'

Once she was nestled in his arms he said, 'I can see it's going to take me some time to convince you just how much I love you, but it'll be fun for both of us, I promise. I think I can do it more effectively when I have more time, so how about a long, long honeymoon? I want to learn what you're like in all your moods—sleepy, grumbly, playful, wicked…especially wicked.'

'Kingsley—'

'Say yes, Kingsley.'

'But—'

'Yes, Kingsley.' He kissed her, his mouth demanding her submission, his tongue circling and stroking. He raised his head, aware as well as she was that she was melting against him, her breasts swollen and her nipples hard and puckered against the rasp of his shirt. 'Yes, Kingsley,' he repeated again, the blue eyes holding hers.

'Yes, Kingsley,' she breathed against his mouth. 'Yes, yes, yes.'

'A quick wedding.' He kissed her again. 'Very quick. Yes?'

'Yes.' She was achingly aroused.

'Mmm.' He shifted position slightly, his own arousal rock-hard. 'I've found the perfect method to get my own way.'

The rain was thundering down now, a virtual torrent, causing the taxi to crawl along, but Rosalie didn't care. The storm had broken but she was safe. She would always be safe with Kingsley. He loved her and he understood her, and that was precious. So very precious. He had been worth waiting for.

'Never doubt my love for a moment.' His voice was thick with desire. 'Never. All the doubts, all the fears, we'll deal with them one at a time, together. You're not alone, my love. Whilst I've breath in my body I'm yours.'

She clung to him, wishing they were alone rather than in a taxi in busy London streets. But there was all the future to be alone together; it stretched, bright and wonderful in front of her eyes, dazzling her.

She could give this man all the love she had stored up in her heart because he wouldn't hurt her, they were bound by forces that had brought them together and would keep them together. One beating heart in two bodies.

EPILOGUE

IT WAS a simple wedding, but none the less perfect because of it.

The bride looked radiant in a pale silver dress created from chiffon and lace, and she carried a bouquet of delicate orchids, their fragile petals just touched with pink and threaded through with silver ribbons. Kingsley couldn't take his eyes off her, the love shining out of his face making all the women cry, especially one or two who had harboured vain hopes in their voluptuous bosoms.

The September day was one of brilliant sunshine, and after the reception for family and friends at a lush London hotel there was dancing until late in the night under the stars on the landscaped lawns, the champagne continuing to flow until the last guest retired.

Kingsley had planned a three-month honeymoon in various exotic places, but that night, he'd said, they were going somewhere special. They left the last of their guests still dancing and slipped away together to the limousine Kingsley had waiting, the uniformed driver resplendent and the car seeming to stretch forever as they climbed inside, Rosalie giggling with excitement and champagne.

'Where are we going?' Rosalie felt as though she were in a dream, a dream she never wanted to wake up from.

'Wait and see, Mrs Ward.' Kingsley's eyes were brilliant in the dim light. At some time during the night he had undone his bow-tie, which now hung either side of his unfastened collar, his jacket slung on the seat of the car. He looked hard and dangerous and breathtakingly handsome, and but for the driver she knew she would have ripped his clothes off on the spot.

She lay cradled in his arms in the car as they kissed, their breath intermingling, but when she asked him, plaintively, how long it was going to be before they were alone, he laughed and told her to be patient.

'I can't be.' She turned her face up to him, rubbing her hand over his lower body beneath the concealing folds of her dress. 'I want you.'

She felt his flesh leap and smiled into his eyes as his hand came out and caught hers. 'Temptress,' he muttered huskily. 'Do you want me to take you right now in the back of the car?'

'I wouldn't mind.'

'Well, I would. Our wedding night is going to be long and slow, and I'm going to spend all night showing you how much I love you, and in comfort. I want to touch and taste and explore over and over again.'

The throbbing ache in the core of her that his words had aroused was just penance for her earlier teasing.

When the car stopped Kingsley had been kissing her for a while, voluptuously enjoying her in the warm velvety darkness as he'd used her submissive mouth to slowly build them both to peaks of arousal, and so she glanced up in surprise, flushed and bright-eyed.

'Kingsley, this is…' Her voice trailed away as her eyes widened.

Beth and George had sold up and were due to leave for New Zealand the very next day after the wedding, and Rosalie had been sad at their going, part of her knowing she would miss the sanctuary of their exquisite old house as well as her aunt.

'Yours.' He finished her sentence, before opening the car door and pulling her out. After he'd dismissed the driver they walked to the front door through the perfumed darkness of the garden she had thought was lost to her for ever, and then he was opening the door and pulling her into the hall. 'We wanted a house in England, so why not this one you love so much?' he said softly. 'It's all empty for you to furnish as you like, except for the master bedroom, which I've furnished for us for tonight, but you can change it if you don't like it.'

'Oh, Kingsley...' Words failed her. She wandered out into the sleeping garden at the back of the house before they went upstairs, the velvet sky overhead with myriad twinkling stars and the scents and smells of the wonderful old garden reminding her of the first time Kingsley had come here with her.

And then they went upstairs, and she gasped with delight at the bedroom as he opened the door. The bed was luscious and huge, a magnificent wicked piece of wantonness with soft, billowy covers and pillows galore, one third at the head of it surrounded by carpeted shelving for books or tapes or magazines. The colour scheme was gold and cream, the carpet thick enough to sink in, and the beautiful cream and gold drapes at the window drifted in the slight breeze from the sweet-smelling garden below.

A TV the size of a small cinema—to Rosalie's fascinated eyes—took up one corner, the door to the *en suite* open and showing a wonderful bathroom following the same colour scheme as the bedroom.

'So this is why Beth and George moved into rented accommodation and packed all their furniture off to New Zealand weeks ago?' Rosalie turned round to Kingsley, who was watching her with laughing eyes. 'Oh, darling, what can I say? How can I find words to tell you how much I love you?'

'You don't have to.' He reached out for her, his hands

moving over the perfect loveliness of her as he whispered huskily, 'You've the rest of your life to show me, my darling.'

Her gaze moved to his mouth and she wondered how she could ever have thought it was ruthless. It caressed hers and she closed her eyes, her slight silver frame fitting into the hard, lean darkness of the man she loved with all her heart.

He kissed her heavy eyelids, one after the other, and then her ears, her throat, before returning to her mouth. He undressed her slowly, pouring kisses on every part of her flesh until she was quivering with a need that made her tremble as she undressed him.

He was already hugely aroused, and his impressive maleness caused an involuntary arch of anticipation as he drew her towards the epicurean bed. This was her husband, her love, and in spite of all that had happened in her past she felt as eager and awestruck as a virgin.

He admired and loved her with his eyes, his hands and his mouth, his boldness calling forth an uninhibitedness she wouldn't have thought herself capable of. His tongue, his hands were magic, and as he continued to pleasure her he did things no one else had ever done and she knew she had been waiting for him all her life without knowing it. He was part of her, wound into her bones, her blood and her heart.

Pleasure coursed through her, focused on the places he touched with such loving precision. He seemed to read her mind, to know what she wanted next, what gave her the most pleasure at just the right moment, and she was conscious of thinking she just hadn't known it could *be* like this. This was joy and bliss and erotic fulfilment beyond her wildest imaginings...

'I love you, my darling. We're going to go on and on

and it's going to get better and better. Do you believe that?'

She couldn't believe anything could be better than what she was experiencing right now. She reached her arms to him, drawing him up and over her as she said, 'Please, please…'

He waited no longer, possessing her so completely that their oneness was the only living thing in the universe, every cell and fragment of her body filled with passion and pleasure and him.

This was her life, her future. This was her love.

Modern Romance™
...seduction and
passion guaranteed

Tender Romance™
...love affairs that
last a lifetime

Medical Romance™
...medical drama
on the pulse

Historical Romance™
...rich, vivid and
passionate

Sensual Romance™
...sassy, sexy and
seductive

Blaze Romance™
...the temperature's
rising

27 new titles every month.

Live the emotion

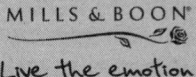

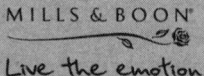

MILLS & BOON

Live the emotion

Modern Romance™

THE BILLIONAIRE'S CONTRACT BRIDE *by Carol Marinelli*

Zavier Chambers is one of Australia's most powerful playboys, and to him Tabitha appears to be the worst kind of woman. Tabitha isn't a gold-digger – but she does need to marry for money. When Zavier blackmails her into marriage she has no choice…

THE TYCOON'S TROPHY MISTRESS *by Lee Wilkinson*

Daniel Wolfe is not a man to be messed with – and he already has an agenda of his own. Charlotte Michaels soon finds herself being offered an unexpected career move – as her boss's mistress!

THE MARRIAGE RENEWAL *by Maggie Cox*

When Tara's husband returns after five years, she is willing to give him his divorce – but not until she has told Mac about what happened after he left. Mac is stunned, but he's as consumed with desire for her as he ever was. Is their passion a strong enough basis on which to renew their marriage vows?

MARRIED TO A MARINE *by Cathie Linz*

Justice Wilder was badly injured while saving a child's life – and now may be facing the end of his military career. Kelly Hart tracks him down in order to convince him to accept help for the first time in his life. But what happens when he discovers she used to love him…?

On sale 3rd October 2003

Available at most branches of WHSmith, Tesco, Martins, Borders, Eason, Sainsbury's and all good paperback bookshops.

0903/01b

FREE

4 BOOKS
AND A SURPRISE GIFT!

We would like to take this opportunity to thank you for reading this Mills & Boon® book by offering you the chance to take FOUR more specially selected titles from the Modern Romance™ series absolutely FREE! We're also making this offer to introduce you to the benefits of the Reader Service™—

    ★ FREE home delivery   ★ FREE gifts and competitions
    ★ FREE monthly Newsletter   ★ Exclusive Reader Service discount
        ★ Books available before they're in the shops

Accepting these FREE books and gift places you under no obligation to buy; you may cancel at any time, even after receiving your free shipment. Simply complete your details below and return the entire page to the address below. *You don't even need a stamp!*

YES! Please send me 4 free Modern Romance™ books and a surprise gift. I understand that unless you hear from me, I will receive 6 superb new titles every month for just £2.60 each, postage and packing free. I am under no obligation to purchase any books and may cancel my subscription at any time. The free books and gift will be mine to keep in any case.

P3ZED

Ms/Mrs/Miss/Mr ....Initials ....
                                                              BLOCK CAPITALS PLEASE

Surname ....

Address ....

....

....Postcode ....

Send this whole page to:
UK: FREEPOST CN81, Croydon, CR9 3WZ
EIRE: PO Box 4546, Kilcock, County Kildare (stamp required)

Offer valid in UK and Eire only and not available to current Reader Service subscribers to this series. We reserve the right to refuse an application and applicants must be aged 18 years or over. Only one application per household. Terms and prices subject to change without notice. Offer expires 31st December 2003. As a result of this application, you may receive offers from Harlequin Mills & Boon and other carefully selected companies. If you would prefer not to share in this opportunity please write to The Data Manager at the address above.

Mills & Boon® is a registered trademark owned by Harlequin Mills & Boon Limited.
Modern Romance™ is being used as a trademark.